THE TOFF AND
THE TOUGHS

THE TOFF AND THE TOUGHS

by JOHN CREASEY

WALKER AND COMPANY

New York

CONTENTS

1

THE DELEGATION

IT has often been said that the Honorable Richard Rollison, known to so many as The Toff, has a sixth sense. There is no way of proving it, although Jolly, his manservant, counsellor, and friend, will testify to some remarkable coincidences. Most remarkable of all, he declares, is the frequency with which Richard Rollison looks out of the window of his flat when something or somebody in the street is coming to see him. It is like a kind of telepathy or thought transference; a theory which is made more reasonable, perhaps, by the fact that nearly everyone who is coming to see the Toff is thinking very hard about him.

On that lovely clear evening late in winter, Rollison was sitting at his desk, and Jolly was picking up the tea tray. No one except Jolly believed that Rollison often worked extremely hard, on behalf of this committee or that cause; in fact the days when he had been an idle young man-about-town were long past. This evening, he was making a report for a Central London branch of the Prisoners' Aid Society—for he kept in touch with many men after they had been released from prison.

Suddenly he put down his pen, raised his head, and looked towards the window. He had something of the manner of a pointer then; it was as if he scented visitors. He pushed his chair back, stood up, stretched and moved casually towards the window. Standing close by the wall on one side of it he could see much of the street.

It was nearly dark, but there was light enough to see clearly. On the other side of the road were four young people, and obviously they were not local residents. Two of them looked as if they were trying to ape Marlon Brando, and the girls had long hair, very short, tight skirts and thin if shapely legs. It was as if four Beatniks had come together in unholy union.

"Jolly," called Rollison. "Come and see what you make of this bunch."

"At once, sir," Jolly said. He put the tray down on a corner of Rollison's desk and approached sedately. Jolly was a head shorter, not quite so lean, and not quite so broad as Rollison. He was twenty-five years older, and his grey hair made that obvious. Rollison's hair was still jet black except for a few treacherous streaks of grey; and Rollison's profile, as he peered down at the quartette, was quite remarkably handsome. The half smile which curved his lips made that much more noticeable. In such moments he looked like a musical comedy hero.

"Think that brood's coming here?" he asked.

"I am inclined to hope not, sir," said Jolly.

"Oh, I don't know," said Rollison. "Something must go on inside their heads. Ah!"

Until that moment four people had been standing together in a huddle, looking at one another. Suddenly, they straightened up as if resolved on a unanimous decision, and the two with their backs to 22g Gresham Terrace turned round. All four stepped into the street, all four looked up at Rollison's lighted window, and strolled across the road; it was interesting that the two girls were in the lead.

They passed beneath a street lamp, and the faces of the girls showed small, pale, and pretty. Then all of them disappeared, while Rollison moved away from the window and picked up the telephone. Jolly, who had served him for over twenty years, had never got used to the speed of Rollison's movements; now, he began to dial almost before the instrument was at his ear. Jolly picked up the tea tray again as Rollison said:

"That you, Bill?"

A man named William Ebbutt, another old friend of the Toff and in his way as remarkable, answered from the East End gymnasium which he had made famous.

"Mr Ar, for a pound!"

"You've won your pound," agreed Rollison. "Do you think you could—"

"Now that's what I call a remarkable thing," interrupted Ebbutt, who had the richest of Cockney voices, and a pronounced wheeze. "I was only saying to Lil this last dinner time, I was saying to Lil, it's a long time since we've heard from Mr Rollison, must be a coupla months, I was saying." Ebbutt pronounced months as 'munce'. "And how *are* you, Mr Ar? Anything I can do for you?"

"I'm fine," said Rollison, "and I'm not sure whether you can help or not, Bill. Have you any rumours that a quartette of youngsters is coming to see me?"

"What kinda young, Mr Ar?"

"Late teen-age, I should think," said Rollison.

"Can't say I've heard nothing about no Teds," said Bill Ebbutt, after a moment or two for reflection. "I can make a few hinquiries, if that would help."

"I'll let you know," Rollison said. "Thanks, Bill, and give my love to Lil." He rang off, before Ebbutt could launch the long series of questions undoubtedly on his mind, and as the front door bell of this top floor flat rang. Almost at the same moment, Jolly re-appeared. Rollison nodded towards the door which led to the hall, and followed Jolly. In the long, narrow lounge-hall, furnished with a small bureau, two easy chairs and with some beautiful mezzotints on the walls, everything was silent. Jolly and Rollison looked up at a small mirror above the door. This was built into the wall on the periscope principle, so that the four teenagers were shown standing outside, slightly distorted and in miniature.

Rollison and Jolly looked for and noticed exactly the same thing; all four had their hands in sight. Visitors with their hands in their pockets had been known to come here to rough the Toff up, and both he and Jolly had learned to be careful.

"I'll be at the desk," Rollison said. "Bring 'em in and then let them wait here for a minute."

"Yes, sir," said Jolly.

By now, many visitors would have become impatient, but not these four; they did not ring the bell again. Rollison sat behind his desk, picked up the pen, then swivelled round in his padded armchair and touched the hempen hangman's rope which adorned the wall behind him; he brought it forward a few inches, and ran his fingers round the inside of the noose, to make it more circular than oval. As he did so, Jolly opened the front door, and said:

"Good evening."

There was a moment's pause; to Rollison it seemed like a pause of embarrassment. Then:

"Is this where Mr Rollison lives?" a girl asked.

"We mean, the *Toff*," a boy blurted out.

"He knows who we mean," put in the second girl; only the second boy kept silent.

"If you will come in, and tell me your business, I will find out if Mr Rollison is at home," said Jolly, his tone at its mellowest; no duchess could have been greeted more resonantly. Rollison heard the rustle and shuffle of movements, and a cough, before a youth said uneasily that they would rather tell Mr Rollison in person what it was all about.

"Very good, sir," said Jolly, and after a moment Rollison's door opened and Jolly appeared. Had he noticed anything even remotely sinister or suspicious about the four he would indicate it by a gesture or come forward to whisper; he looked slightly puzzled and actually shook his head. "Mr Rollison," he said so that the four could hear, "four young persons have called to see you, sir."

Rollison paused long enough to make sure that the four stayed on tenterhooks, and then asked:

"What about, Jolly?"

"They preferred not to say, sir."

"Do we know them?"

"No, sir."

"Have they any introductions?"

"No, sir."

"Hm," said Rollison, and wished he could see the expressions on the faces of the waiting visitors. There was no shuffling outside, and the silence suggested that they were listening intently. "I'm not expecting anyone for the next half hour or so, am I?"

"No, sir."

"Then show them in," said Rollison.

He was rising from his chair as the four appeared, and it was obvious on the instant that they were indeed embarrassed. Three of them—two men and the blonde girl looked straight at him. The brunette glanced at him for a moment, then past him to the rope and to the other remarkable articles on his Trophy Wall. He saw this girl's eyes widen, her lips parting momentarily; she wasn't exactly a beauty, but attractive and well-poised, with a beautiful olive complexion.

"Mr Price, sir," Jolly said, and moved a hand towards all four, "and his friends."

"Hallo," said Rollison, and rounded the desk. Price appeared to be the taller of the two youths, each of whose over-long hair was combed straight back from his forehead, both of whom affected shaggy sideboards, fancy waistcoats, jackets which had been slept in, and stove pipe trousers. "What can I do for you?" Rollison asked, and held out his hand.

Price said: "*Very-good've-you-to-see-us-Mr Roll'son,*" in a strangled voice; but his hand was cool and his grip firm and rather eager. "*This-is-Missevens-Missdarby-Misterly.*" It took Rollison several seconds to realise that the introductions really covered Miss Evans, Miss Darby and Mr Lee, and he shook hands gravely in turn. Only Miss Evans's hand was warm and a little sticky; she was the brunette who had stared at the Trophy Wall.

Now that the moment of meeting was over, the other three wanted to look anywhere but at the Toff, so they also settled for the Wall. It had a hypnotic effect on most people who had not seen it before, but this was the first time Rollison had known it serve as a salve for embarrassment. He watched two pairs of grey eyes, one pair of sky blue, and one pair of hazel brown as they switched from one item to another on the Wall—from a .33 pistol to a stiletto with a brown-tinged tip; from a jemmy to a sword-stick; from a silk stocking with a dab of red nail varnish on it to a box of test tubes each containing deadly poisons. There were many more such exhibits, and the Curator of the Black Museum at Scotland Yard had been heard to say that he resented being second best to anyone. The gaze of all four visitors finally rested on a top hat above the rest of the trophies; the Toff's top hat, with a bullet hole through the crown. This even superseded the fascination of the rope.

All four visitors looked back at Rollison at last, who smiled and said:

"Ominous-looking little lot, isn't it?"

"Ducky," the blonde said.

"*Fas*cinating," declared the brunette.

"They all yours?" demanded the taller lad.

"In a manner of speaking, yes," answered Rollison, when he was sure that the second youth did not intend to speak. "They all belonged to bad men, and I tangled with them. They gave me those as souvenirs."

"Some souvenirs!" exclaimed the tall youth.

"They *gave*?" inquired the blonde elf.

The youngsters were beginning to register as individuals on Rollison's mind, and while at first they had appeared to be remarkably similar, except in height and colouring, now there were noticeable differences. The blonde's face was round and she had a country girl's rosebud complexion, glorious blue eyes, a face so full of eager promise that it was a ludicrous anti-climax to see the flatness of her bosom and the thinness of her legs; she was the shortest of the four. The brunette was a head taller, yet not very tall; she had the hazel brown eyes, and Rollison had an impression that these were more intelligent than those of the others. She had a narrow face, the smooth

olive complexion, a pointed chin, a black stockingette
sweater which was pulled high round the neck; and no one
could complain that she wasn't well-endowed with statis-
tics. The long jumper stretched down over her narrow
skirt, showing that she had slender hips, and that her legs
were nearly as slim as the other girl's. Price, the taller
youth with the firm handshake, was on the dark side, on
the pimply side, on the concave side; weedy or willowy,
according to one's charity. The silent, shorter one wasn't
quite a blond. He was stocky, his shoulders were very wide,
stretching the jacket at the seams, and in spite of his
appearance and shabbiness, he gave an impression of
considerable physical strength. His grey eyes were guarded
by very long, curling lashes.

"May I sort everyone out?" asked Rollison, easily.
"You're Mr Price"—the tall one nodded—"Mr Lee?"
The other jerked his head once. "Miss Evans?" The
brunette with the warm hand said: "Yes, that's right," and
the blonde gave a bewitching smile, and finished for him:
"I'm Anne Darby."

"Well, sit down," said Rollison. "And what will you
have to drink? It's a bit late for tea, but—"

"Oh, we don't want anything, Mr Rollison," interrupted Anne Darby, and it was becoming increasingly
obvious that the brilliance and sparkle of her eyes could
make it easy to forget that she had such a boyish figure.
"We've come to ask a favour of you, we don't want to im-
pose." She glanced at Price, who was busy moistening
his lips, and went on impatiently: "Alec—Mr Price—
is—"

"Oh, *you* say it, Anne," said Miss Evans.

"No, it's all right," said Price, ridding himself of his
vocal paralysis. "Mr Rollison, we—er—we—ah—we've
all heard such a lot about you and we wondered if—
didn't we, you chaps?—we wondered if you'd lend us a
hand doing a job—er—we know it's the kind of thing
you're supposed to be interested in and we'd be really
grateful if you'd lend a hand. Lend us your name, as a

matter of fact, that's really all we want." He was perspiring very freely. "We aren't after your money or anything like that, I don't mean, we'd say no if—but what I mean is, what we would like is—"

He broke off, gulped, drew the back of his hand across his forehead, then looked at Anne Darby with such poignant appeal that few could have refused to come to the rescue. She had probably been waiting for this tongue-tied moment, and jumped in with almost embarrassing promptitude.

"What we want to do, Mr Rollison, is to raise funds for a new kind of organisation, and we believe that if you'd help us to get started your name would get us a lot of publicity. All we need is a start."

She said that as if she were absolutely certain that once they had their start, success was assured.

"I see," said Rollison, non-committally.

"We know you'll have to be told much more than this," went on Anne Darby, "and we're really just a delegation from the others. If you'd agree in principle to helping, provided we could satisfy you that we're worth it, that's all we need."

She stopped.

"Tonight," put in Alec, hurriedly. "I mean, that's all we need tonight. I mean—"

"He knows what we mean," said the brunette, drily. "Don't you, Mr Rollison?"

2

PURPOSE

ROLLISON studied the four faces in front of him, and questioned whether he had ever seen greater intensity; it was as if all of them were willing him to do whatever they wanted. He wondered what Jolly was making of this; Jolly was undoubtedly at the door which led to the domestic quarters, listening, so that later he could give Rollison the benefit of his opinion. If the delegation meant exactly what Anne Darby and Alec Price said, there could be little harm in saying that he was interested enough to want to know more, but—did they mean only what they said? The young could be innocent, but none could be more cunning. Rollison could imagine another side of this picture: a group of high-spirited teenagers, spiced with malice, setting out to make a fool of the man who called himself the Toff; scheming, in other words, to bring him toppling from some imagined pedestal to humiliate or to make ridiculous. Neither of these possibilities troubled Rollison; the act of allowing himself to be deceived would annoy him, that was all.

He could not help feeling that the two girls were more purposeful than the men. Then he thought: "Men!" and had to smother a grin.

"What we mean—" Alec began, as if he felt that he had to rescue a lost initiative.

"I think you mean that you'd like to take a message back to say that if the proposition looks legal and reasonable I wouldn't mind backing it with my name and a few guineas," Rollison said.

"That's it exactly!" cried Price, as if such reasoning were from an oracle.

"I really think you should all sit down, have a drink, and tell me more about this," said Rollison. He stretched

15

out and pressed a bell beneath the side of his desk; and as
if by magic, Jolly appeared. "We'll need some ice and
water, Jolly, and I think . . ."

The two young men settled for beer; Doris Evans for a
lager; Anne Darby, with a gleam of apology, for a bitter
lemon. "I always get tight on a couple of sips of gin," she
confessed, and smiled as if she knew Rollison would appreciate the absurdity of that. Instead of putting them on
edge, Jolly put them all at ease, and soon they were sitting
in the large room in a half-circle about Rollison's desk,
Rollison acting chairman in his chair, Price and Lee—
Jonas Lee—sitting in armchairs, the girls on upright chairs
which enabled Doris to nurse her knees and so show
Rollison what lovely legs she had. Anne tucked her legs
beneath her chair; her knees looked tiny as well as nylon
smooth. Doris and Price smoked cigarettes, Lee and Anne
did not. Everything Rollison saw suggested that these
were absolutely genuine; and eager, too.

As if by natural right, Anne began the talking.

"I daresay you think we're idiotically young and immature, Mr Rollison, and perhaps we are, but we're sick
and tired of being blamed for everything—well, for nearly
everything. If you listened to all the pronouncements of
the educationists and the moralists you'd think that
youth today was the one blot on civilisation—sexually pro-
miscuous, indecent, criminal, out for what they can get,
all that kind of tosh. And when anyone wants to take us
in hand they start a club in which we're supposed to do
everything that our elders think we like. It so happens I
don't like ping-pong, cards, physical training, jolly concert
parties or sewing classes, but that doesn't mean I'm a
cretin or a juvenile delinquent or a natural whore. The
truth is, if any of us moves out of the rut, we're called
Beatniks or Teddy Boy-Girls, and *decent* teenagers won't
have anything to do with us. Ma and Pa are shocked.
Well, Ma and Pa might be even more shocked if they knew
that we think they've brought Little Willie up to be a pan-
headed idiot. Do you see what I'm driving at?"

"He would have a job to," remarked Doris Evans.

"*Do* you, Mr Rollison?"

"You can be different and still be human," Rollison murmured, tritely.

"Eight words to your two hundred and seven, and he got there quicker," said Doris.

"Doris, *do* shut up."

"Dry up, Doris," Price urged.

For a moment Rollison thought that Jonas Lee was going to speak, but all he did was to give Doris a look that was half appeal and half frown, and then stare at Rollison as if recalling the oracle.

"If we have a club," Anne said, "we want to run it ourselves, and we want it to cater for ourselves and other people like us. We also want to finance it ourselves. I suppose what we're really trying to say, Mr Rollison, is that we want to show everyone that we're perfectly capable of running our own affairs without charity, condescension, or moralising. The trouble is that whenever we start we run up against stiff-necked mutton-heads who won't admit that we're serious. We have difficulty in renting premises, for instance. If we want to book a hall for a dance we're told to get references—even our money isn't good enough."

Rollison had to grin. "Nobody loves you."

"That's about it," agreed Doris Evans.

"Why come to me?" asked Rollison.

"We need a name and we need a figurehead," answered Anne, "and that's *exactly* what I mean. You've got a bigger reputation than anyone else in your own sphere, and you earned it by being unconventional and doing what you thought was necessary your own way. If you'd listened to the police, I daresay half of those souvenirs wouldn't be on that wall, you might even be dead by now. *You* snapped *your* fingers at the police, and as a result the police come and consult you these days." After a pause, she added naively: "They do, don't they?"

"It has been known," agreed Rollison gravely. "They no longer think I'm a bad man."

"That's exactly it," said Anne. "We want to prove that even if we wear black stockings, cut our hair so that we look like over-grown golliwogs, and hoist our skirts above our knees, we're *people*. My hat, when you see what comes out of the beauty *salons* sometimes you'd think all women were becoming titivated tarts! Yet because we don't slap on paint—"

"Dry up," Doris Evans interrupted.

Anne stopped; and all four studied Rollison with that eager intentness which had characterised them from the moment they had entered. He was amused and even intrigued, still a little wary in case they were taking him for a ride, although not at all averse to helping if this was genuine. But it mustn't appear too easy; at most he could encourage them to hope that he might see this thing their way.

"How many of you feel like this?" he inquired.

"Oh, at least a hundred," answered Price. "We're all from the Chelham Technical College—that's practically a University College but we haven't been elevated so high yet. All of us come from the same kind of background—"

"Nonsense," interjected Anne.

"Dammit—"

"From the slums up to suburbia, you see," Doris Evans said. "What Alec really means is that none of us is county or public school or—"

"Cases of inverted snobbery are worse than the straight jobs," Rollison said mildly. "Are you planning to do this through the college?"

"Not a chance," answered Alec. "That's really where the trouble began, Mr Rollison. There's a Students' Society, of course, and a year or so ago it was healthy and flourishing—it raised a lot of boodle for charity in the annual rag, and did all the usual things. Then some of us wanted to get a bit off-beat and we clashed with a capital A for Authority. Yes, sir," went on Alec; obviously this was the subject closest to his heart, and he became much more confident. "The Principal disapproved of some of the floats we were preparing for last year's Rag Procession. He disapproved, the Chelham Council's Education Committee disapproved, a couple of our chaps got tight at a Rag Ball and were held up as the Awful Example. We were given a specific schedule of what the S.A.—"

"Students' Association," interpolated Doris.

"—could do and couldn't do, and the S.A. virtually broke up then and there," went on Alec. "We weren't bound to belong. We found that two or three other colleges were in the same boat. The truth is that the authorities were cracking down hard on anything off-beat run by teenagers, and we felt as rebellious as hell."

"We felt sure you would understand why we wanted to tell authority where to get off," said Anne, earnestly.

Rollison chuckled.

"I daresay I can, but remember I'm in the sere and yellow these days. Exactly what do you want me to do?"

"Wish we knew," said Anne.

"*Some*thing *diff*erent!" declared Alec.

"We don't want to worry you with all our brilliant ideas," said Doris. "If you said you'd help us, we'd go back to the others and hammer out a policy, then get you to vet it. That's if you wouldn't mind."

"I can't see myself leading a revolt against the Education Committee of Chelham Borough Council," Rollison said, and at once saw the disappointment which shadowed the faces in front of him. "I can't see myself leading a teenage crusade, either. Boss of the Beatniks wouldn't exactly fit me as a position or title." He stopped and contemplated them, and had seldom felt so sure about young people. They were acutely disappointed because they thought that he was going to turn them down, and if they could be so disappointed, this surely mattered to them as a cause. "However," he went on mildly, "there might be another way of handling the situation."

Anne's eyes blazed, Alec's face lit up, Doris gave the slow, rather droll smile which seemed to characterise her, and Jonas Lee clapped his hands together resonantly enough to startle Rollison.

"Good-o!" he exclaimed.

Apparently this outburst was normal, for none of the others turned to look at him.

"What way, Mr Rollison?" inquired Anne, looking quite angelic.

"Well, supposing I started something and you joined me," suggested Rollison, and before any one could interrupt, he went on: "And don't say that isn't the idea until you've heard the rest. I've a lot of interests—here's a report on two chaps who served three years for robbery, for instance, and were released six months ago. They report to the nearest police station according to the law, but I'm a kind of Unofficial Probation Officer for them. It works fairly well. Or there are the Limehouse Louts, a club run in conjunction with a gymnasium owned by a friend of mine in Whitechapel. The roughest and toughest East Enders belong: in fact unless you're tough and unless you've been up before the magistrates you can't belong to it."

"That's different, anyhow," conceded Doris. "What would we have to do to join? Break windows? Pick pockets? Or—"

"The Limehouse Louts wouldn't look at you," Rollison declared. "Black stockings to them are as red rags to bulls. But you could come up against something run more or less like that. For instance—"

He hesitated; and although he no longer looked straight at the delegates, he could tell that they were anxious, still slightly disappointed, not at all sure that he wasn't fobbing them off. He opened a drawer on the right of his desk, took out a folder, and opened it in front of them.

"This might be the answer," he said, thoughtfully.

"What is it?"

"Not another *club*?"

"If you're serious, we'll have a crack at anything," Anne said.

"Oh, I'm serious," Rollison assured her, and placed his right hand, palm downwards, on the papers inside the folder. "Here's one nut I've never been able to crack. The police haven't either. These people are as hard and tough as young human beings can be—they don't come any tougher." He made a little drumming sound with his fingers on the papers, looked from one to another until he judged that he had teased them enough, and went on: "It's a group of teenagers from fifteen to nineteen—a few are in their early twenties—mostly as vicious as wild animals. There must be twenty-five or thirty of them altogether, and the worst are all that's brutish and un-social in teenagers and Teddy Boys. It's people in this kind of group which get the rest of you into disrepute—youngsters like these are really the cause of your problems, not the principals of technical colleges or the committees which run the schools. A few of these youngsters are really bad. Some people say they're born bad, and maybe that's true of some of them. But they're not all congenital cases, and—"

Rollison broke off.

"What would you expect us to do?" asked Alec Price in a hopeful voice.

"Alec, love," said Doris, sardonically, "the Toff is hoisting us with our own petard. He's offering us the opportunity of becoming great social reformers instead of being reformed. I think it's very clever, Mr Toff." She smiled across at Rollison, and those honey-coloured eyes seemed to become tawny and sleepy. Inviting? It would be easy to believe so. "Aren't I right?"

"Yes," said Rollison.

"How would we go about it?" demanded Anne.

"Some time in the next week or the next month this mob is going to cause trouble," Rollison said. "They'll beat up some defenceless old couple for a few pounds, or they'll jump a copper doing his job, or steal a couple of cars and crash them. Anything for what they call excitement. It will be sure to hit the headlines. I've friends in the Press who will quote me if I let rip, and say that they're utterly beyond control, like all young people today, blah-blah. Then you can jump in. Bring a protest march with banners along Piccadilly and Gresham Terrace, carrying banners saying what you've just said: you're sick of hearing young people blamed, these youths I've been damning are as good as the next, it's my generation which is wrong. Get the idea?" he asked, and looked intently from one to the other.

It was Alec Price who said: "Yes, I think so, Mr Rollison. But wouldn't this be pretty dangerous? I mean—*couldn't* it be?"

"Of course it could," murmured Doris. "Mr Toff wants to find out how soon we'll get cold feet. It's a very clever way to get rid of us. Isn't it, Mr Toff?"

That was the second challenge she had offered in that gentle and yet mocking way of hers.

"Nonsense," said Rollison. "I give you the chance, and you take it or leave it."

"But how—?" began Alec.

"Do you really want me to do your thinking for you?" demanded Rollison. "Is that why you came?" When none of the others answered, he went on cheerfully: "You'll get a lot more public attention by slapping me down than by following my lead."

"And don't you mind being slapped down?" inquired Anne.

"It's happened before and it will happen again," said Rollison. "And with this Whitechapel mob, it ought to be interesting to find out what happens when someone stands up for them instead of joining in the usual hate campaign."

"But should we defend a really brutish mob?" asked Doris.

"Good question," said Rollison, "but the point is that you will think this mob has been wrongfully maligned—as you have."

"That answers *that*," rejoiced Price. "But how can we keep up to date with all sides of the situation?"

"There's no reason at all why we shouldn't work together under cover—you let me know when the protest march is going to be staged, and I'll make sure I'm here, for instance. When it's over we can hold another council of war." He looked round, and saw that all their eagerness was back, with the possible exception of Doris Evans's. She appeared to be very thoughtful. "Right?" he asked.

"Good-o!" cried Jonas Lee. "That's for me. Up the Toff."

"Don't you mean 'Down With the Toff'?" inquired Doris, sweetly.

3

THE SLOB MOB

ROLLISON did not take the delegation too seriously, but on the morning after the visitation, he walked briskly through a London incredibly beautiful in a kind of Indian Winter. It was February. The crocuses and the snowdrops were nodding in the Royal parks, and the daffodils were spiking upward as if they meant to stab the sky. No one took particular notice of Rollison, except two policemen and a newspaperman who recognised him. He walked first through Green and then through St James's Park, and found Parliament Square crowded with sightseers and politicians; something special was on that day, and he remembered the visit of an Eastern potentate, a nice old-fashioned touch. He walked on the north side of the square, turned round by the Embankment, and half-an-hour after leaving Gresham Terrace he was sitting in the office of Chief Superintendent William Grice, his old friend, his old adversary—and the man who knew more about the Toff than anyone except Jolly.

"Nice morning," Rollison remarked, looking out of the window upon the beauty of a blue Thames spattered with diamonds, and the County Hall where all the flags were flying.

"You didn't come to talk about the weather," Grice observed. "What do you want, Rolly?"

"Kind words and a little guidance," Rollison said.

"When you come to me for guidance, that will be the day," scoffed Grice. Sitting behind his desk he looked as if he would be very tall—he was—and his broad shoulders were smooth in a close-fitting suit of dark-brown serge. His hair was brown, although grey was taking over, and his skin was sallow. His high-bridged nose was white at the bridge itself, where the skin stretched very tightly, and his chin was curving and pointed. One side of his face had an ugly scar—from a burn which had probably done more than any other single thing to make these men close friends; for they had been involved together in an investigation when Grice had nearly been killed by an explosion. Rollison had been able to save his life. "What are you after, Rolly?" Grice demanded. "I don't want to be uncivil, but this is a day of days. Every man we've got is out in the streets, in case some lunatic tries to throw a bomb at the Prince of Alsa."

"Bad as that?" inquired Rollison.

"Don't be so hopeful. No. It's a lunatic fringe risk, that's all, and we have to watch for it. Any moment the A.C. might ring up and tell me that I've got to do this, that or the other job, so—"

"How is the Slob Mob these days?" inquired Rollison.

"Had trouble with them?"

"No."

"Keep away from the Slob Mob," advised Grice earnestly. "They get worse instead of better, and one of these days there's going to be serious trouble with them. All they need is a leader who can give them a sense of power and keep them together. Why the interest?"

Rollison was about to explain when one of the telephones on Grice's desk gave a long, explosive burst; and something about it warned Rollison that this was the half-expected and urgent summons. Grice lifted the receiver, listened for a moment, and said:

"Yes, sir. At once." He put the receiver down and stood up at the same time. "Not the Assistant Commissioner, but the Commissioner himself," he announced. "They've caught a couple of Alsa rebels in Whitehall. Sorry, Rolly. This problem can wait, can't it?"

"Why not?" asked Rollison.

There was no point in explaining a little, so he said nothing, shook hands, and watched Grice striding along the corridors towards the Inspectors' Room. Grice might be one of the big shots here, but when the Commissioner of the Metropolitan Police barked, Grice jumped.

Rollison went outside. The crowd near Parliament Square was even greater, and television and newsreel cameras were trained on the spot where the Prince of Alsa's car was likely to be. Rollison crossed the Yard in the other direction, went across Cannon Row and into Parliament Street, where the crowd was not so thick. Then he walked back towards Gresham Terrace. He was a little uneasy, although it would have been impossible for him to explain why. It was another manifestation of his sixth sense—all was not as well as he would have liked.

*　　*　　*

He and Grice were not the only people giving some thought to the Slob Mob that day.

In the East End of London, living among the hundreds of thousands of Cockneys whose lives were quite as good, moral, and natural as the lives of the masses in the better residential districts, were the inevitable misfits. Heredity, environment, and living costs all contributed to the fact that there were more social misfits in this part of London than in any other, and Harry Pyne was one of them. Very few people knew Harry Pyne, for very few had reason to. He was the sixth child of a family of nine, his father—now dead—had been a dock labourer, his mother—now re-married—had been a hard-working, hard-swearing, hard-headed woman who had wasted very little time on Harry, because even from early childhood he had seemed able to look after himself. Among her large family he had been a solitary kind of child; had she not known better, his mother might have believed that he had a different father, but Mrs Pyne had been as physically faithful as a woman could be.

The truth was that she had never liked Harry very much. Even as a baby he had disliked being kissed.

Few people since had ever really liked him, he was such

a cold fish. His hands were always chilled, yet usually a little damp. His pale face had no expression in it. His big eyes—remarkably big, nearly black eyes—never looked quite alive. He was not a big man, nor was he really small. He had a long narrow face, a high, narrow forehead, and his shoulders were slightly rounded, so that he had a permanent stoop. Very few people had ever discovered the truth about Harry Pyne: from the time that he began to reason, he had known what he wanted, and had always been prepared to wait for a long time in order to get it—and also, to make sure that no one could take it away. If necessary, and if he felt sure he would not be found out, he would commit any crime; even murder.

He had a genius, too, for getting things the easy way.

For many years he had known that he wanted to be the leader of one of the London gangs, but there had been many obstacles in the way. For one thing, most of the gangs had leaders who could wield much more influence than Harry Pyne. These were youths who had a leader's personality, could sway a crowd, could command loyalty by their personality. Pyne's genius did not lie in that direction. He realised this, and knew that he was essentially an administrator. He wanted to take over a gang, not create one; and at the time of the takeover the gang had to be in urgent need of what he could give them. He had the sense to realise that he would need a front, or a voice—someone who would be the ostensible leader but who would take instructions from him. It was the awareness of his own power and authority, the sense of importance that these would give him what he wanted, rather than the trappings of leadership.

For some months—perhaps for some years—the Slob Mob had seemed likely to offer him all this.

Years ago, it had been a big gang, well led by a dynasty of big shots, but for some time its power and its authority in the East End had been on the wane. There was no real figurehead, and more important, there was no intellectual drive, no planning, behind the Slob Mob. Its members met together in various parts of the East End, but most of its raids were sporadic, and almost the only thing which really held it together as a unit was trouble for any of its members with the police. That was where Harry saw his opportunity. The members could be united under threat from outside—so they could be welded tightly together, given the right leader.

For a long time, he had been looking for this figurehead; and now he had found him, in Ginger King.

He had been watching Ginger for some months, since his return from a three years' visit as Her Majesty's guest. When he had come out Ginger had been fierily vengeful in spirit, mature in body, nicely immature in mind. His grudge had been against the police—not against Pyne, who had lured him into crime. He had a big, round, handsome face, he could smile engagingly, and people liked him. He had a carrying voice, and could shout down anyone he wanted to, and also had great powerful fists, but absolutely no physical fear. Pyne was quite sure that Ginger King's basic trouble was that he could not think for himself; he had never been able to think a step ahead of anyone. Yet the Slobs both liked and admired him; properly trained, they could be made to follow him blindly. Ginger had been on the fringe of the Slob Mob for many years, and Harry Pyne had been right in the centre of it, saying very little. Then he had pulled Ginger right in.

Only last week, Harry had talked to Ginger, who had swallowed the spiel at one gulp. Someone was needed to pull the mob together, and who better than he? Sure, he could do it. And he would! Just call them together, and he would talk to them. Why hadn't he thought of it before?

Harry Pyne knew.

Pyne also persuaded him that it would be much better to wait until circumstances brought the mob together, than to summon them. For weeks, Ginger had been mixing with the various factions in the mob, getting himself well-liked, spending money—much of it Pyne's money—with reckless generosity. A hero fresh from prison, he was more popular than he had ever been, and Harry knew that the time had come for a crisis to be engineered. He needed three or four of the toughest members of the group to do something which would really bring the police down on them. Once united in enmity to and hatred for the law, they would call for a leader. Harry would be able to tell Ginger exactly what to do.

The crisis had to be caused by something that would hit the headlines, bring the police down on them, and at the same time soon die a natural death. Murder was out, for instance. Attacking a cop was out too, because the police had particularly long memories where one of their own number was concerned. Raiding a shop was out. The kind of thing which fitted in perfectly with Harry's idea was a gang war—not very vicious at this juncture, just something to get everyone's hackles rising. So he worked very hard, sifting all the information that he could, until he discovered that there was some internal trouble in Slash Taggarty's gang, in Bethnal Green.

There was a little rebel group in Taggarty's Gang, half-a-dozen members, each with his girl, and this seemed to fit in perfectly with Harry Pyne's ideas. He knew the Taggarty Gang's habits. The men met, to drink and gamble, early in the evening; the girls joined the men later, when the serious business was finished. They always met at a converted warehouse near Bethnal Green Road, where they had dancing to a stereophonic radiogram. Harry Pyne knew that the six girls attached to the rebels always went along together, knew about what time they would reach the dance hall, and knew the best place to intercept them.

* * *

The six girls, nicely made up, expensively dressed, although too loudly, with ridiculously high heels, absurdly narrow skirts, close-fitting jumpers and fuzzy-wuzzy hair, tap-tapped along the pavement towards the dance hall two evenings after Rollison had received the delegation. They were laughing and talking among themselves, and in their way were happy. Each knew that her boy friend was having a spot of bother with Taggarty, and that added to the spice of life. None of them really cared which boy friend she had, provided she had one; they were young, amoral and amorous, and curiously innocent in outlook. It did not occur to any of them to be afraid of dark corners, and only one glanced up at a gas lamp fastened to the wall—which usually showed a pale light, but tonight was in darkness. In a bunch, listening to one girl telling a highly Rabelaisian story of what had happened to her and her sister, they turned the corner.

Before they had time to scream, Harry's chosen members of the Slob Mob fell upon them; Harry had given instructions very precisely. There were six youths, each of them with pieces of adhesive plaster all ready to slap over their victims' mouths; only two stifled screams escaped before the plaster was pressed down hard. Then the girls were methodically stripped. It was a bitterly cold night following that spell of sunshine winter, but first their coats, then their jumpers, then their skirts, then their underclothes were peeled off them. They stood in shivering terror, eyes glistening in the distant light. Then, with speed and skill, their hands were tied behind them and they were all roped together, and made to run, barefooted over the icy pavement, along the street, round the corner to the 'dance hall'. By a strange irony, a small group of Salvation Army 'lassies' were canvassing in the street at that very moment. They stood, shaken and shocked, as two of the Slob Mob banged open the doors of the hall. The others drove the six girls inside, and after the first screams of horror, there was a deathly silence. The Salvation Army party knew that this situation was beyond them, and sent for the police.

*　　　*　　　*

By the time the police knew, Harry was saying to Ginger King: "There's going to be trouble tonight, Ginger; if I was you I'd start putting a warning around. Okay?"

"Okay," said Ginger King, as if he had thought of the idea himself.

4

PERFECT JUDGEMENT

HARRY PYNE's judgement of the consequences of the stripping incident was absolutely perfect. Once Taggarty had realised whose girls had suffered, he had to struggle hard not to split his sides with laughter, and yet the pride of the gang had been affronted, so there had to be at least a token raid on the Slob Mob, who met in the Whale Street Club. This was an old barn of a place to look at, once a flourishing Youth Club but broken up by the gangs. Before the raid was properly under way, word reached Taggarty that the Slob Mob was massed together in the yard of a disused factory near the river, not in Whale Street. Fifty or more hard-eyed, vicious young toughs made for the factory, but before there was any real fighting, the police arrived in squad and Q cars and even a Black Maria. Whistles shrilled out on the frosty night, headlights shone on the fighters, breaking off their engagements and running for cover. Half-a-dozen prisoners were taken by the police but the rest got away.

That was exactly right for Harry.

When the shouting, the fighting and the running was over, the Slob Mob met again, this time in the run-down club two miles away from the scene of the fight. There they listened to Ginger King telling them what they had to do next. If they didn't stick together, travel in groups, and make sure they always carried a knife, cosh, razor, piece of iron piping, or bicycle chain, they would be at the mercy of Taggarty's Mob. So they would have to travel in groups of five or six and make sure they couldn't be attacked singly, each look after his own chick; they all had to do everything that Harry Pyne told them through Ginger—and Ginger could put the ideas into words with a vigour which really made an impression.

"Only thing I'd have had different is this," he shouted, clapping his big hands together. "All I wish is we'd *all* been there to see that nudist race! Jeese, what a sight for sore eyes! Can't you imagine them running, all their bubs . . ."

The Slob Mob dissolved into lusty laughter, and by the end of the evening they were convinced that there had never been a better leader than Ginger King. No one seemed to notice that when they broke up for the evening, Harry Pyne went off with Ginger. Too many police were about, stationed at various vantage points, for there to be the slightest danger that night; everyone could feel sure that they would not be disturbed—the next night or two would probably be very quiet. There might be another attack from Taggarty's, soon, but Harry's information was that Taggarty would probably tell the six outraged boy-friends to look after their own tarts; and if that happened there would be internecine strife in Taggarty's.

In fact, that started the next night.

And the evening papers carried the story that night, too.

*　　　*　　　*

When Rollison first heard what had happened from a newspaperman whom he had tipped off to keep an eye on the Slob Mob, he began to laugh. He could picture in his mind's eye the line of running nudes, urged on by their attackers; it would have needed a modern Hogarth to draw the picture in all its comic wildness. He laughed; Jolly smiled; the newspaperman chuckled. Grice came on the telephone, laughing a little grimly, wanting to know whether Rollison had realised what was going to happen.

Rollison said lightly: "No, Bill, and if I had I don't think I could have lifted a hand to stop it. The girls weren't hurt, were they?"

"Hardly a scratch," said Grice.

"None of what is technically known as interference?"

"A few slapped bottoms and a bit of slap and tickle, all in high spirits," said Grice. "I don't mind admitting it looks like tearing the Taggarty Gang apart. They were one of the worst we've had to contend with for a long time, and it won't do any harm. We're going to watch those two gangs so closely that—"

He broke off, said: "Just a minute," and then came back and spoke hurriedly. "Sorry, Rolly, we've had a report in about a double murder in Wimbledon. I'll be seeing you."

He rang off.

Rollison hung up, thoughtful but still smiling, and looked across at Ray Harrison, one of the livelier reporters of the *Evening Globe*. Harrison was twenty-eight, looked twenty-two, and could see the funny side of most things. He had curly hair and an angelic kind of face, reminding Rollison slightly of Anne Darby. Harrison had come to Gresham Terrace at a word from Rollison, hoping for a story.

"What's the official view?" he asked.

"Grice sounds more relieved than sorry," said Rollison, "and apparently the Yard's had one of its more raucous laughs."

"Nothing like a bit of ridicule to make a mob like Taggarty's mob pipe down," said Harrison. "What's your angle?"

"Moral righteousness," said Rollison.

"You've changed!"

Rollison chuckled. "I want to lend a hand with some youngsters . . ." he began, and outlined to an attentive Harrison the basis of the delegation's visit, and what the four had wanted. Obviously Harrison relished all this. "So if I let rip on the iniquity of youth, this will let them in," Rollison went on. "I can't think of a better thing to shout about. No one was hurt, it wasn't much more than a bit of rough horseplay. If I wax righteous about what a shocking thing to happen and all that kind of thing, some of my friends might wonder what I'm up to, but it should work the wanted miracle. Can you quote me?"

"Gladly."

"And will you see that the Protest March is reported?"
"By all of Fleet Street and both television outfits,"
Harrison promised. "What shall I quote?"

*   *   *

YOUTH OUTRAGES ITSELF—SAYS THE TOFF
SHAMEFUL EXHIBITION OF BRUTALITY—SAYS 'TOFF'
THIS CAN ONLY END IN LOWERED MORALS—*Toff*

In all, he had seven front page and three inside pages
in the London newspapers, and twenty-seven people rang
him up to ask if he had suddenly been converted. Among
these, quite as eager as the delegation, was Lil Ebbutt,
Bill Ebbutt's wife. For years she had been a militant cap-
tain in the Salvation Army, and her 'girls' had been at the
scene of the outrage. The Toff was noncommittal. For
the whole of the next day he waited, hearing nothing from
Alec Price or any of the others, and he had a sense of
having been let down; if the teenagers were going to take
him up on this, they would surely have told him by
now.

It was a little after five o'clock, and still daylight, when
he put down the telephone after a talk with a friend who
advised him to go on holiday, stood up, and sauntered
towards the window. Jolly was not in the room. Rollison
reached the spot where he had been when he had first
seen the quartette—and quite suddenly the quiet of
Gresham Terrace was broken by the boom of a drum. At
first he saw nothing, but suddenly the drum boomed out
again, and a band chimed in—bass and drum, banging
and booming, playing a medley which became louder and
more confusing every second; and suddenly the head of a
procession came into sight, the leaders carrying a huge
banner which read:

COME ORF IT, TORF

Rollison pushed up the window, and leaned out. The
drums boomed. Jolly came hurrying, but Rollison did not

hear him; he could only hear the chant which came above the sound of music:

"COME ORF IT, TORF!"

Behind the first banner were others: LEAVE YOUTH ALONE; LET YOUTH LIVE; WE'RE OLD ENOUGH TO FIGHT FOR YOU; GOING SOFT, TOFF? There were others, carried by banner-holders swinging round the corner, one boy and one girl at each pole. Between each banner a group of twenty or thirty marching youths, led by a brass band which was at least forty strong. They came swinging along Gresham Terrace and it had never been so outraged in all the time that the Toff had lived here. The singing and the shouting was subdued, and the marchers began to slow down. Rollison realised that they were forming up outside Number 22g, making a wide half circle; but they were being very cagey. There was room for traffic to pass behind them, a path for one lot of pedestrians behind them, too, but the rest of the street was chock-full of teenagers, some dressed fairly well, most as Beatniks, the girls with their hair conjured into strange shapes, with high-necked sweaters, knee-length skirts. Those knees were going up and down, up and down, as they marked time to the tune of the band, which was playing the tune of I'M GETTING MARRIED IN THE MORNING. But they were not singing the original words: gradually the lyric was borne to the Toff's ears:

Why Don't You Go and Take a Jump, Toff,
Why Don't You Shut Your Silly Mouth?
Who Wants to Hear From an Old Frump, Toff?
Why Don't You Shut Your North and South?"

"This is rather more than you anticipated, surely," Jolly said, speaking very close to Rollison's ear so as to make himself heard.

Rollison chuckled.

"More and better," he said. "The young devils have taught me that they can do plenty for themselves. I wonder—look, Jolly, there's the BBC Outside Broadcast Unit —and an ITA News cameraman. The youngsters laid it on all right, and even Harrison didn't tell me when it was coming."

Jolly said: "Surely the police will soon come."

"Yes, they'll break it up," Rollison agreed, a little regretfully. "It looks to me as if the mob gathered round the corner and didn't start the procession until a few minutes ago. It's a very slick piece of organising. Can you see—?" he broke off, for he caught sight of Anne Darby and Doris Evans, while not far away was Alec Price. He couldn't see Jonas Lee, but Jonas might easily have got lost in this crowd. Rollison made a rough count, reached the total of fifty, and judged that there were at least four hundred teenagers in the street. Undoubtedly Jolly was right, it wouldn't be long before the police came to break things up. He clenched his fist and shook it—and the singing and the music stopped, there was a roar of derisive laughter. He shook his fist again. The television cameras were turned on him, now, and there was another gust of laughter, followed, as if rehearsed in perfect unison, by:

"COME ORF IT, TORF!"

"Really, sir," said Jolly, "I find it quite embarrassing."

"You wait until you see the morning's newspapers," said Rollison, and then saw heads turning towards the far end of the street. Someone shouted: *"Take it easy, here are the cops!"* The youths were really keeping their heads, Rollison reflected, they weren't going to risk a clash with the police, and for a big crowd of teenagers worked up to this pitch, they showed remarkable self restraint. The band struck up. The paraders turned and began to march towards the far end of the street. The banners were waving and passing the Toff's window. The cameras, perched on top of the vans, followed skilfully, raking all of Gresham Terrace and never missing the Toff. A few policemen in uniform, with two sergeants, followed at a smart pace, as if their sole job was to make sure that the marchers kept on the move. There wasn't a single incident, as far as the Toff could judge. The band turned the corner, the music stopped, the chanting stopped; apart from the sound of marching footsteps of those who were still in the Terrace, there was quiet.

Ray Harrison passed the window, and waved to Rollison.

"If I may say so, sir," said Jolly, "I think I should be very careful indeed about giving that young person advance information. At the very least he should have warned you."

"He's nearer their age than mine," Rollison remarked philosophically. "With a bit of luck, that's touched all the ego they need touching, and given them the safety valve they needed. A good time was had by all. I—"

He was still by the window, seeing no need to back away. The marching party was past him, and only a few were looking back. A straggly crowd of children and elderly people with a few policemen mingling, trailing along like camp followers, were looking up at Rollison, and he was smiling to himself as they passed. Then out of the corner of his eyes he saw another crowd turn into the street in the wake of the camp followers; the first individual he noticed was a big, tall youth with flaming red hair, who looked like a kind of General Teddy Boy trailed by his camp followers.

Quite suddenly, this group broke into a run. Rollison judged that there were at least fifty of them. These youths were not older than the Beatnik mob, but their Teddy Boy clothes made them look it. Next to the ginger-haired man was another, narrow-faced, with a high forehead and eyes which seemed to glitter, even from here; and it was he who spoke to the red-haired man, who raised his voice in a single bellowing sentence:

"*Let 'im have it!*"

Suddenly every man's hand appeared from behind his back, as suddenly the air was filled with potatoes, tomatoes, oranges, stones, pieces of brick. As they crashed against the wall and against the window, Rollison realised exactly what had happened. He heard a stone crack glass; heard the breaking of more glass at the flat below. An orange smashed on the window sill and splashed all over his hands, a potato thudded against the window frame, and he saw the skin split, saw the yellowish inside, saw the razor blade which stuck, scintillating and quivering, in the window ledge. Then another potato caught him a glancing blow on the forehead, and he felt the sharp pain of a razor blade cutting the skin. He backed away. A tomato plopped on the window sill as Jolly reached the window, and tugged at the cord which controlled the curtains; it was like Jolly to realise so quickly that the curtains would save both the room and the furniture from greater damage.

Outside, police whistles sounded shrill and urgent, there were bellows and catcalls and the sound of more breaking glass.

Rollison turned towards the door of the room, saying:

"You stay here, Jolly. If anyone telephones, say I'm out." He strode across the lounge hall, and only at the last moment did he glance up at the periscope mirror. It was a good thing that he did, for two youths stood outside, one on either side of the door; and in one youth's hand was a length of bicycle chain.

5

BLAME?

ROLLISON stopped short, some distance from the door.
His footsteps had been muffled by the carpet, so there was
no fear that he had been heard; the men outside might
have heard him call out to Jolly, but that was all. He
spun round, and almost cannoned into Jolly, who was
following him. He whispered: "*Tear-gas, quick*," and on
the instant Jolly turned round. Rollison went after him,
past the kitchen door, past the bathroom and into Jolly's
room, which was part bedroom, part laboratory, and even
had a corner which he could use as a dark-room. Nearly
everything likely to be needed in emergency was kept
here; it had been Jolly who had installed the periscope
mirror, and Jolly who had declared that a few little phials
of tear-gas might occasionally save them a great deal of
trouble.

He had never been more right.

He opened a drawer in an oak tallboy, took out a small
wooden box, opened it, and held it towards Rollison, as if
he were offering cigarettes; the phials in it looked like
cigarettes, although they were made of thin painted glass,
not of paper. Rollison took four.

"Thanks," he said, briskly.

Police whistles were still shrilling in the street and he
could hear the sounds of the fighting, but he paid that no
attention as he went towards the door. This time he
called out in a loud voice:

"Lock up after me, Jolly!" By craning his neck even
when he was close to the door, he could see the two youths,
grinning, raising their weapons to strike. He put his right
foot against the door as he opened it, making plenty of
noise so that the pair knew exactly when to expect him.
They would plan to wait until he stepped out, of course,

and then savage him. He opened the door only a few
inches, and tossed one phial out. He heard a startled ex-
clamation, and the men outside tried to push the door
shut, but it banged against his foot and swung back in
their faces. As it opened again, he dropped another phial.
He heard them gasping, heard a metallic sound as a
length of chain fell to the floor. He took a deep breath,
narrowed his eyes, stood to one side and pulled the door
wide open. The two youths were staggering helplessly on
the landing, their hands at their eyes; and the sharp gas
stabbed at Rollison, too. He grabbed one arm of each
man, twisted, and yanked them inside; they could do
nothing to save themselves. He twisted again, sending
them hurtling against the wall; one man fell, the other
pitched over him.

Jolly said: "I can look after them now, sir. Be careful
downstairs, won't you?"

"Very careful indeed," Rollison promised.

So far, he had had little time to think, only to act and to
react. Now he stepped across the landing, pulling the
door to, and started down the staircase; he did not have
carpet on the flight near him, because the stone echoed
footsteps more clearly. The front door was ajar, sealing
off most of the sound from the street, and there was no
sound in the house itself. He could see each landing, and
there was nowhere for strangers to hide. He reached the
next landing, watching the doors; there was just the possibility that the Slob Mob had taken over a flat, if necessary
holding the tenant prisoner. No door moved. He reached
the last landing. Rollison wondered if anyone was on the
porch, took out two more of the tear-gas phials, and repeated the manoeuvre that he had performed upstairs,
except that this time he did not toss out a phial.

No one was on the porch, but a uniformed man was
turning towards it. Across the street, another uniformed
man lay on his side, with blood coming from a wound in
his forehead. Two youths were lying huddled by the curb.
Three mounted policemen, appearing as if from nowhere,

trotted along Gresham Terrace, and two of the riders glanced towards Rollison. He opened the door window, and the policeman said:

"Mr Rollison?"

"Yes."

"Are you—" the man began, and then drew in a deep breath. "That cut!"

"It's just a scratch," Rollison said. "I was at the window and the razor blade caught me. How are things?"

"Didn't take long to drive them off once we started," said the policeman, and then Rollison saw several newspapermen and cameramen. Lights flashed, spools whirred, and it would be useless to try to avoid them. One man called out: "How bad is your head?" Rollison stepped closer to the pavement and looked along the street. Several teenagers were standing about the open doors of a Black Maria, and climbing in at the orders of several policemen. None of the original delegates seemed to be there, and all of the prisoners looked like the Slob Mob. A big, harsh-voiced newspaperman called out:

"What's your view on teenagers now, Rollison?"

"Going to get your own back?" a spindly man called.

"What action would you recommend?" demanded the hard-voiced man. "You in favour of birching?"

"How about the cat?" a youngish woman called. "Don't you think that is the only answer to these hooligans, Mr Rollison?"

Rollison stood watching and listening as if blandly, but he didn't speak. He caught sight of Harrison, some distance off, but the young man from the *Evening Globe* came no nearer.

"For Gossake, say something," the harsh-voiced man said.

"I think our police are wonderful," murmured Rollison, "and I could also tell you what I think of our Press."

"Come off it, Rolly!"

"Let's have something to quote."

Rollison said: "For every teenager who would bury

a razor blade in a potato, there are a thousand who would rather eat fish and chips. Who's the officer in charge?" he asked a uniformed sergeant.

"Detective Inspector Nicholson, sir, from the Division."

"I don't think I know him."

"Even the Toff can't know everyone," jeered the spindly man.

"Don't you think the part which the girls played was disgraceful, Mr Rollison?" the sweet-voiced woman demanded.

"Girls?" asked Rollison. "Were there any girls?" He looked at the sergeant. "See if Mr Nicholson can spare me five minutes, will you?" he asked. "I'll wait at my flat." He turned round and went inside, knowing that cameras were still whirring, knowing also that he was puzzling some of the newspapermen. That in itself did not trouble him. He was beginning to feel and to think—and also beginning to wonder just how far he was to blame for what had happened. A great number of people would say this would never have taken place but for him; in this particular way and in this Mayfair street, that was certainly true. There were other causes for anxiety, too. He went slowly up the stairs, reached the top landing, and smelt the sharp tang of tear-gas. He opened the landing window wide, and slipped into his flat. The entrance hall was empty, and there was no sign of any damage. He had a moment's fear; that there had been more razor-flashing youths at the back entrance, and that Jolly had fallen to them; but Jolly appeared, immaculate and unscathed in his black jacket, striped trousers, and his cravat.

"I think you should have that forehead dressed, sir," he said.

"Soon. There's a copper named Nicholson coming round, from the Division," Rollison said. "Where are the hoodlums, Jolly?"

"Together in the brush cupboard, sir."

"Looked after?"

"They will be quite immobile for some time."

"Good. No reason to think that this Nicholson knows they're here." Rollison led the way to the bathroom, looked at himself in the mirror, and widened his eyes. "I see what you mean." The razor blade had nicked the skin for about four inches and the scratch had bled profusely; blood was caked on to the lower part of his forehead, too, on his eyebrows, and even on his cheeks. "I'll wash that, you get the honours ready for Nicholson—we want him in a good humour if we can."

"Very good, sir," Jolly said.

Rollison took off his jacket, rolled up his sleeves, and washed his forehead. The blood had congealed hard and tough, and he had to use soap and not a little pressure. The scratch was deeper than he had thought, and painful, but when he rubbed a healing salve in, the pain quickly eased. There was a slight swelling on his left cheekbone, where some missile had struck him, and his hands were covered with dried tomato juice. Otherwise, he was all right. He went into his bedroom, changed quickly into a pair of slacks and a knee-length dressing gown-cum-smoking jacket, and went into the big room as the front door bell rang. Jolly went to open it; and as he did not pause before actually opening the door, Rollison knew that this was the police—or someone trustworthy, anyhow. A man spoke in a deep voice which seemed to place him at once:

"Is Mr Rollison here?"

"Yes, sir," said Jolly. "May I tell him who—"

"I'm Detective Inspector Nicholson," the man announced.

"This way, sir, please," said Jolly.

Rollison was standing by the window when Nicholson came in, and his first glimpse of the man was not at all encouraging. He did not think that Nicholson would have much sense of humour or even of proportion, and felt quite sure that his attitude was likely to be censorious. He was alone; that was something.

"Hallo, Inspector," Rollison welcomed. "Sorry that I've sparked off this kind of shindy."

Nicholson said at once: "So you admit that it is your responsibility, sir."

Rollison thought: 'Oh, Lor'.' Nicholson seemed even more likely to be one of the less imaginative policemen, prejudiced against all 'amateurs' and looking for a scapegoat. Rollison moved towards the open cabinet where bottles glowed in many colours and hand-cut glasses sparkled. Nicholson did not look at the drink, but at Rollison, who stopped by the cabinet.

"I wouldn't put it quite like that," he said. "I didn't send out invitation cards, you know."

"There is very little doubt that this riot was the result of your remarks as reported," Nicholson declared.

"Ah," said Rollison. "Possibly." He picked up a bottle of Johnnie Walker. "If you combed the newspapers for every magistrate, retired policeman, and earnest social worker who said pompous things in a moment of pique, would you blame them for any ensuing riot?" he demanded. "How about a drink, Inspector?"

"Not now, sir. Mr Rollison, I would like you to answer a number of questions, and consequent upon your answers I shall make my recommendation to my superiors."

He really was a stiff-necked ass, Rollison thought, and longed for Grice.

"Carry on," he said, outwardly quite affable, and poured himself a nip and splashed in soda. "You won't mind if I have a drink, will you?"

"You are perfectly at liberty to do as you wish, sir. Were you aware that this protest march would be organised?"

Rollison said: "I had heard rumours."

"Did you know when it was to take place?"

"I did not."

"Are you sure, sir?"

Rollison sipped his drink, glanced down at the whisky and soda, looked up at Nicholson, who stood solid and massive and utterly unimaginative; he wasn't a bad-looking man, and would probably do very well in the scrum, even better as a wrestler.

"Yes," Rollison said, "I am quite sure. And Mr Nicholson, I do not like being called a liar, by implication or in any other way."

"No offence intended, sir."

"I trust not. What else do you want to know?"

"Had you arranged for the gang from Bethnal Green to be present?"

Rollison said: "Good God, man, do you think I've gone mad?"

"I did wonder, sir," said Nicholson, flatly. "I was informed that you believed that by bringing these two groups of young people together you thought that it would be possible to bring about friendship and understanding. Isn't that so?"

"You could put it that way."

"Are you—" began Nicholson, and then as if he saw the gleam in Rollison's eyes, he changed even the tone of his voice as he went on: "Had you been in touch with either party earlier in the day, sir?"

"No."

"At any previous time?"

"I've seen members of both parties," Rollison said, "and I hope I shall again."

"What is that remark intended to mean, sir?"

Rollison said: "You're fairly new to this part of the world, Inspector, aren't you?" When Nicholson stood silent, he added: "I think you might check with some of your colleagues who know me rather better, and ask them what they think I mean."

"I intend to, sir," said Nicholson. "I think you should understand, Mr Rollison, that I shall urge that the most effective action possible be taken to make sure that you do not attempt to take personal vengeance upon your attackers. There is no reasonable doubt that indirectly or directly you were the cause of this disturbance, and—"

"Mr Nicholson," said Rollison, gently, "I'm very busy. Do you mind leaving?" He put his glass down, smiled

pleasantly, and walked to his desk. He pressed the bell—
and Jolly appeared with his uncanny promptitude.
"Show Detective Inspector Nicholson out, Jolly, will
you?" said Rollison, and Jolly murmured something
under his breath, while Nicholson stood solid, a little
baffled, but still stubborn. He moved towards the door
while Rollison stood at the desk, smiling at him.

"You ought to know better than to start a thing like
this," he said, roundly. "You ought to know there's no
way of telling where it will end. If I have my way, you
won't be able to do any more harm."

Rollison simply beamed at him. Nicholson hesitated,
then turned round as if willed by Jolly, and went out.
The sound of footsteps was followed by the opening and
deliberately sharp closing of the door. Rollison sat on a
corner of the desk until Jolly returned. He was wondering
what Nicholson would have said had he known about the
two prisoners; even more significantly, he was wondering
about Nicholson's censorious attitude as a whole, and
about that final burst of feeling when the man had taken
over from the policeman.

"Shall I get you a drink, sir?" asked Jolly.

"Yes," Rollison said. "A double whisky, and I'll finish
the one that's poured out. Hear all that, Jolly?"

"It is a great pity that an officer with such an outlook
has to be in charge of this situation, sir."

"I know it," said Rollison. "I don't like the chap any
more than you do, but can either of us say that he's not
right?" Jolly brought the half-empty glass, and Rollison
tossed the whisky and soda down, watched Jolly pouring
out another, and went on: "Quote. 'Once this kind of
thing starts you can never tell when it's going to end.' End
quote. How right he was. That's enough soda, don't
drown it!" He waited as Jolly came across with the drink,
and then forced a smile as he said: "Thanks. Key
question, Jolly—who told the Slob Mob what was going
to happen? Secondary questions: who is the ginger-
haired chap who was leading the mob, and who was his

first lieutenant? We want to get Ebbutt busy, but we ought to make sure that no one starts taking sides.''

"Shall I call Mr Ebbutt, sir?'' asked Jolly.

"Yes.''

"Very good, sir,'' Jolly said, and went across to the telephone, touched the receiver and was about to lift it when the bell rang. He paused for a moment, then lifted the instrument and announced in his normal manner: "This is Mr Richard Rollison's residence.''

Rollison was close enough to hear the words which crackled from the receiver.

"Tell the bloody Toff he's asking for it. If he doesn't let my pals go inside the hour, he'll wish he'd never been born.''

6

CHECK

ROLLISON heard the words 'wish he'd never been born', and on the 'born' he made a gasping kind of sound, startling Jolly, who turned his head sharply and nearly lost his grip on the telephone. Rollison took it from him, and as he put it to his ear the man at the other end of the line shouted: "You let them go!"

"Ah," said Rollison. "Mr Slob, I presume?"

"If you don't let . . ." the speaker began, and descended into threats and obscenities which told their own ugly tale. Rollison let him finish, then said mildly:

"None of this will help you or your friends. I'll send them back when I'm ready, and it may not be for hours. If any more of you come here, if any telephone me again, if any of you attempt to attack me or my staff, I shall hand your pals over to the police, complete with bicycle chains."

"*Knives!*" whispered Jolly.

"And knives," Rollison continued smoothly. "That will mean three years inside, at least. I have a scratch across my forehead which might be construed into attempted murder, that would take it up to seven years. Good evening."

"Listen, you—"

Rollison rang off, drew his hand across his damp forehead, and made the deep scratch sting. He stood up from the desk, took a cigarette from a silver box on it, and lit the cigarette from a book of matches. Jolly was standing quite still, as if awaiting instructions.

"Check, I hope," Rollison said.

"I can't imagine they will attempt anything while we have the two prisoners, sir."

"I hope not. Are they conscious?"

"Oh, yes."

"We'll talk to them," said Rollison. "We'd better use your room, Jolly. Nicholson might come back with reinforcements, and I'd hate to be caught with battered bods all over the flat. Jolly."

"Sir."

"I want to be quite sure that I don't put a foot wrong again. Both feet have been in the wrong place far too often already. I should have taken your advice, and told Alec Price and Company that I only played ball with grown-ups." He smiled faintly. "Wasn't it Doris Evans who asked me whether I minded being slapped down?"

"That was the young woman, sir."

"So she slapped. And let's face it, they laid on this march and everything else very efficiently."

"In my considered opinion, they had help from some-one much more experienced," Jolly declared.

"You mean, older people?"

"Yes, sir."

"I wonder," mused Rollison. "And I wonder if you aren't making the mistake that a lot of adults do—forgetting that these youngsters may be much more capable of running their own affairs, and organising big occasions, than we believe. When you come to think of it, a lot of my own club members don't exactly inspire confidence, do they?"

"I see what you mean, sir," said Jolly, in a tone which revealed his complete disagreement. "Shall I ring Mr Ebbutt now?"

"I'll call our Bill," said Rollison. "You go and check with that pair of slobs." He lifted the telephone and began to dial as Jolly walked off, his shoulders very straight and his manner deliberate. He heard the ringing sound. It was now past opening time, and Ebbutt would be in his pub, the Blue Dog, not in the nearby gymnasium where many of London's best fighters were trained. At last, Ebbutt himself answered, sounding breathless as if he had been running.

"Bill—" began Rollison.

"Mr Ar!" exploded Ebbutt. "You okay?"

"I'm fine, Bill."

"The lousy lying slobs, they told me you'd been took to 'orspital," Ebbutt said disgustedly, and sounded almost as if he were disappointed. "Sure you're okay? Not 'urt at all?"

"Scratched, Bill. Bloodied but unbowed, as they say. How did you get to hear of it?"

" 'Ow wot—cor strewth, Mr Ar, it's the only subjeck being discussed, everyone who comes in's talking about it, it's all over the East End. The Slob Mob come back and said they'd made such a mess've your place and your phizzog that you wouldn't show your face again for a coupla munce." Ebbutt drew a deep breath, and when he went on he took much more care with his enunciation and his aspirates. "Is there anything I can do for you, Mr Ar? My chaps are just spoiling to have a go—"

"No, Bill," Rollison ordered urgently. "No reprisals, even if every friend I've got in your manor would like to start clouting Slobs. Make sure no one starts trouble, won't you?"

This time there was no doubt at all that Ebbutt was disappointed.

"If you say so, Mr Ar."

"I couldn't say so more strongly, Bill. This could become really nasty if we let it get out of hand. Do you know the ginger-haired chap in the Slob Mob?"

" 'Course I do. Ginger King."

"Is he the mob leader?"

"Just took over," declared Ebbutt. "Apparently it was Ginger who rallied the mob arter the trouble with the Taggarty Gang." Ebbutt's voice broke into amusement, and he gave himself time to guffaw. "Caw, that was a sight for sore eyes, that was. Funniest thing was, my Lil's gels saw it, and you know what an old sobersides she is. Come tearing round to me with her face as red as the ribbon round her bonnet. I couldn't believe my ears when she told me. The Harmy'd had a Council of War or sunnink, they were just going to invade the Taggarty place with *War Cry* when this Slob Mob crowd come whooping along the street, making those six beauties hop, skip and jump—caw, Mr Ar, if I'd seen it I would have died laughing. As a matter of fack I'm not in the clear yet."

"In the clear with whom, Bill?"

"Lil, o' course. I couldn't help it, Mr Ar, as soon as she told me I burst out laughing. To hear Lil talk, you'd think I'd been helping to pull the bras orf the dearies. I'll tell you one thing, Mr Ar, those chicks won't show their faces for a couple of munce or more. More, I shouldn't wonder."

"You could be right," conceded Rollison. "And after that strip-tease act, Ginger King took over the leadership."

"That's how the story goes," Ebbutt said.

"Know much about Ginger?"

"I know a bit," Ebbutt said cautiously. "He's been inside, three years for beating up a couple of sozzled sailors, and pinching a few quid orf 'em. A lot of people say he liked the fight more than the dough."

"Was he always with the Slob Mob?"

"More-less," said Ebbutt, "but I don't mind admitting I wouldn't have thought he was big enough to be boss, Mr Ar. He's got plenty of nearly everything except little grey cells. Couldn't see any further than his nose when I knew him—useter come to the gym, Mr Ar, got plenty of strength and plenty of guts, but he's a bird-brain."

"There was a man with him, a tall, narrow-faced chap with dark eyes," Rollison said.

"Dunno who that was," said Ebbutt. "Might 'ave been any of them."

"Bill, find out all you can about Ginger, who put him where he is, and what he and the mob's likely to get up to—but keep right out of trouble. Don't let me down, will you?"

"You needn't worry," Ebbutt assured him, and rang off.

Rollison stayed where he was, looking at one of the least likely trophies on the wall—a clerical collar with a brown stain on it which had once been the bright red of blood. Many years ago he had helped a fighting parson in the East End, in some of the ugliest and bloodiest of the London gang wars, and he was thinking of this when he stood up and went to see Jolly's prisoners. Detective Inspector Nicholson was absolutely right: one could never tell where a thing of this kind was going to end, and if Ginger King and the other leaders of the gang were going to try to assert themselves, it might be as bloody as any battles of the past. The raid in Gresham Terrace was a pointer to the mood of the Slob Mob: they would have gained enormous prestige from it, in the East End, and it could go to their heads like raw whisky.

Rollison went into Jolly's room.

Sitting on upright chairs, arms pinioned to their sides and looking like trussed dummies, were the big boys of the bicycle chains. These chains were stretched out on a sheet of newspaper at the foot of Jolly's bed, and by each was a flick knife, small, ugly, lethal. Rollison looked at the two prisoners. Jolly had strapped their mouths as the mouths of the six girls had been, so that they couldn't speak. They were quite different to look at. One was big, chunky, with a battered and swollen right ear, a broad nose, thick lips. He had fair hair which was cropped very close to his bumpy, round-shaped head. His eyes were set rather close together, and they glittered defiance from slate-grey shadows. The other man was taller and thinner, and had a mop of jet black hair which rose almost straight up from his head. He had a very long chin, too. It wasn't the man who had been with Ginger King, but one very much like him in cast of countenance.

"Take that plaster off, Jolly," Rollison said.

Jolly stretched out a hand, to pick at a corner of the tape and to pull, and the chunky man reared back in his chair, as if he knew what it would feel like when the plaster was ripped off.

"Dab on a little alcohol," Rollison said. "We wouldn't want to hurt them, would we?"

Jolly looked at him as if he was talking out of the back of his neck, for Jolly knew this kind of adolescent beast, knew that they understood little more than the weapons with which they themselves fought; and Jolly was undoubtedly feeling vengeful, not only because of the injury to his employer, but because of the damage to the window and the curtains. He did not forgive easily.

"Alcohol," Rollison repeated, firmly.

Jolly stepped to a row of shelves and took down a bottle; and almost at once the sharp odour of surgical spirit invaded the room. He dabbed some on cotton wool and soaked the adhesive plaster, left it for a moment or two, and then peeled the plaster off. All this time two pairs of eyes were turned towards Rollison, as if the two men were trying desperately to guess what was in his mind.

"Got their names?" Rollison asked.

"According to driving licences, sir, the larger man is Wilfrid Smith, and the dark-haired man is named Girodo."

"Ah," said Rollison. "The worst of two worlds." He looked at Girodo, who was obviously of Italian extraction and the one who looked more intelligent. "How long has Ginger King been the Big Slob?" he demanded.

Girodo looked startled.

"Who told you—?"

"Little man," said Rollison, "I get around. Didn't anyone tell you? How long?"

"He—he just took over."

"Who's his right-hand man?"

"Now, listen—"

"Just answer the questions," Rollison said, and his voice hardened, his expression became bleak, and he clenched his right hand into a fist which was very near Girodo's face; he gave the impression that he wanted nothing better than to crash it on to the Italian's nose. "Who's his right-hand man? The man who looks rather like you and sticks to Ginger's side like a clam?" He paused, but Girodo didn't answer, and he unclenched his had and slapped the man's lean face, four times in quick succession, making him draw in sharp breaths, making him try to cringe away. "Now, who is it?" he demanded.

Girodo muttered: "It's Harry Pyne."

"So it's Harry Pyne," said Rollison. "Ginger King and Harry—"

He broke off, for there was a sudden banging on the back door—the door nearest Jolly's room; and almost at the same instant the front door bell began to ring. As that started the telephone bell rang, too, *brrrr-brrrr*; *brrrr-brrrr*. Thudding, banging, raucous ringing all came together, and then to add to the din, men started to shout and a girl began to scream.

"Let us in!" she screeched. *"Let us in!"*

7

BEDLAM

"Take off the receiver, then watch the front door," Rollison ordered, and his voice only just sounded above the bedlam. The ringing kept on and on, the girl stopped screaming—and there were other sounds, a booming on the iron treads of the fire escape which led straight to Rollison's back door. He saw the glitter in the eyes of the man Smith, and felt sure that Smith believed that this was his rescue party. He went out of the room and Jolly followed, calling:

"Sir!"

"Hurry, Jolly."

"Be careful! They—"

"I know," Rollison said, "assault back and front," but he didn't stop moving. He strode into Jolly's immaculate kitchen, where peeled potatoes were standing in a small stainless steel saucepan, and savoy cabbage was soaking in the sink. The booming and banging on the fire escape became much louder, and a man screeched out; it sounded as if a girl was sobbing. Rollison saw that Jolly had shot the bolts top and bottom and fastened the chain. He kicked the bottom bolt back and stretched up to the top one, as a man outside called:

"*Let us in!*"

That was Alec Price.

Rollison pushed the chain aside and kept a foot against the door as he opened it; he caught a glimpse of Alec and Anne, on the platform, and Jonas Lee two steps down, standing like a rock against the onslaughts of half-a-dozen of the Slob Mob who were storming up the fire escape. Jonas jabbed out his right foot and planted his heel in a

56

man's chest, and although the man reeled backwards, the pressure of the others behind him stopped him from crashing down the steps.

"Inside!" Rollison said, and Alec Price staggered past him. Anne followed, trying to gasp out something which Rollison couldn't catch. Then he saw three figures down in the courtyard at the foot of the fire escape; two youths and a girl.

"They've got Doris!" gasped Anne.

Rollison heard and understood in the same moment. Then he saw Jonas Lee draw back, as if he hadn't the strength to hold out any longer; immediately the crowd jammed on the narrow iron staircase surged forward to vicious triumph. As they came, Jonas launched himself forward with the propulsive fury of a rocket, and managed to get a hold on the nearest man's wrist. Rollison saw the man's face writhe in pain, saw the way Jonas heaved him up off his feet, then thrust him bodily into his fellow slobs. The man immediately behind slipped, and fell, and two others toppled backwards. Jonas drew back again, only to hurtle forward, intent on forcing a way past the crowd to the girl below.

Jolly appeared.

Rollison saw the 'cigarettes' in his hand, saw him toss one into the middle of the seething crowd on the staircase. Rollison said calmly: "Watch 'em, Jolly," and turned to the iron railing of the fire escape landing. He gripped it firmly, and swung himself over; for a moment it looked as if he were going to try to jump to the concrete yard forty feet below, but he had played this trick before, and simply swung himself over to the iron platform outside the flat below. He landed square on his feet behind the Slob Mob, then began to run down the staircase. One of the men in the courtyard let the girl go, and came rushing to meet the new threat. Rollison saw the length of iron piping in his hand, knew exactly what to expect, and there was no Jolly here to help him. He found himself thinking that whatever else these members of the Slob Mob lacked, it wasn't physical courage. He raced down, the other man raced up, and they met at the lowest landing. Rollison saw the man swinging his iron piping, and threw himself forward bodily, rather as Jonas had. The piping caught him on the shoulder but didn't stop him. He brought his knee up savagely, caught his adversary, brought a grunt of pain, and heard the piping clatter on the iron staircase. He slammed a fist to the man's stomach and chin, then pushed by.

Above, the other members of the gang were grunting and gasping, and the staircase reverberated and clanged—deafening, menacing. Someone was staggering down them, obviously blinded by the tear-gas. Rollison reached the courtyard. The man guarding Doris Evans swung round to meet him, bicycle chain swishing.

Doris ran forward, and kicked this man behind the knees. He buckled up like a folding chair.

"Nice work, Doris," Rollison said, and jumped forward, to pick up the chain. The man tried to pull it clear, but Rollison planted his heel on the bunching fingers, and the man hissed with pain as he let go. The clanging became louder, the footsteps drew very near, and Rollison saw the rest of the Slob Mob gang spilling out at the foot of the fire escape. They could only just manage to see where they were going, and were running wildly yet with some sense of purpose towards the narrow alley which led to a side street and to freedom. Rollison grabbed Doris, put his arms round her, and protected her against any attack; but the Slob Mob men were now interested only in escape. Even the man whom Rollison had attacked scrambled to his feet and began to run; only the one whom Rollison had fought on the fire escape was still lagging behind. He was at the foot of the steps, clinging on to the rail as if he knew that he could not stand without support.

Then Rollison became aware of Doris, returning his pressure; Doris, her arms round him, holding him very tightly and looking up into his face and smiling. Her lips were parted; she had very white teeth, and they glistened in the light from the courtyard lamps, and from light which streamed out from Rollison's back door.

"Thank you, Toff," Doris said, and strained against him and raised herself on tip toe, her lips inviting.

*   *   *

He could push her away, rebuffing her, and there was no telling what she would do or feel. He could kiss her lightly and casually, as a man might kiss a child or a young girl; but that would not satisfy Doris Evans. He did not yet know what to make of her, but was sure that he wanted her on his side—at least for the time being. He had so little time to think. His fists were sore, his forehead was sore, he was a little out of breath—but he could not be unaware of the pressure of her body, the firmness of her young breasts against him. In a second or two, this moment would be won or lost. Already someone was shouting:

"You all right down there?"

And already footsteps clattered on the iron steps.

Rollison slid his right arm down from Doris's shoulders, and gave her a hug so powerful that he saw the smile vanish and heard her catch her breath; then he kissed her, knowing she was too breathless to kiss back, realising too how unpracticed she was in the ways of seduction. When he let her go, she dropped her arms, dazed, amazed.

"*You all right?*" That was Jonas Lee, and as Rollison turned round, he saw Jonas vault over the railing of the last part of the staircase, and land easily on the concrete. Light still shone out above their heads.

"We're fine," Rollison called. "How are tricks up-stairs?"

"You had me scared," declared Jonas Lee. "Couldn't see what was going on." He looked searchingly at Doris, who had a scared expression now, and who was staring at Jonas, not at the Toff. "Okay, Dorry?"

"Y-yes," she stammered.

"Got another of the swine," Jonas remarked casually,

and looked at the Slob Mob member who was now letting go of the railings, and trying desperately to keep his balance. Jonas strolled towards him, put out a hand, and as casually pushed him down. He went like a log; and as he fell, several policemen came running into the yard.

Immediately, Rollison wondered what would happen if the police found Smith and Girodo, still bound to their chairs.

* * *

Other police had come from the street, here in force after the alarm had been raised, and when Rollison reached the flat he saw Detective Inspector Nicholson standing rather like an avenger, looking at Alec Price, who had been hit over the head and had a bump the size of a hen's egg on it, and at Anne, who seemed small, elfin, and scared. Then he turned his attention to Smith and Girodo, each on his feet, each free of bonds, and obviously released by Jolly. Two uniformed policemen came from Jolly's quarters and reported:

"That's all, sir."

"Right," said Nicholson, and turned to Rollison as if he were about to utter another ponderous warning. Instead, he said: "Are these the only two prisoners, Mr Rollison?"

"There's another down in the courtyard. Your chaps had him cold."

"I see. I would like a full explanation," announced Nicholson.

"I wish I could give it to you," said Rollison. "All I know is that there was a shindy back and front, and when I got to the back door, some friends of mine were—"

"*Friends?*"

"Let me introduce: Alec Price, Anne Darby—"

"You mean these young people?"

"Yes," said Rollison.

Anne Darby said in a rather breathless voice: "Perhaps I can explain, Mr Rollison. We—we were all very sorry about what happened this evening. We'd intended to take the micky out of you, if you know what I mean, but we didn't dream that these others would join in. We were coming round to apologise for any inconvenience, and saw four men—well, four *louts*—creeping into the house. So we rushed round to the back to warn you, but there were half a dozen or more coming that way, too. We just managed to get ahead of them, and warn you, but they caught Doris."

"Doris?" ejaculated Nicholson. "Is one young woman still missing?"

"She's all right now," Rollison soothed, and smiled across at the taller girl, who still had a puzzled and bewildered look. "Aren't you, Dorry?"

"Oh, I'm fine," she said, sighingly.

"What happened to the chaps at the front?" asked Rollison.

"They were warned that the police were on the way, and ran off," Jolly informed him. "I observed them from the hall, sir. The telephone call was from a man who would not give his name, but who uttered certain threats."

"Ah," said Rollison, and waited for Nicholson to say again that there was no telling where these things would end; but all Nicholson said was that he must make a report, at once, and might he use Mr Rollison's telephone? He used the instrument in the big room, while Anne Darby led Alec into the main bathroom, to bathe his head. Alec seemed very dazed and unsteady, possibly from concussion. Anne was studying first aid and nursing, it transpired, while Lee was studying architecture. Alec Price was in engineering, and Doris unexpectedly declared that she was interested mostly in cookery.

Anne seemed glad to discover cuts and bruises on Jonas's hands, and to fuss over them at the kitchen sink, while Jolly switched on an electric hot plate, and placed a saucepan of water to boil. He made no comment about anything that had happened.

Rollison went into the big room, where Nicholson was putting down the receiver.

"Finished?" inquired Rollison.

"For the time being," replied Nicholson, and he looked both bovine and accusing. "I warned you that there was no telling where this kind of thing would end, sir, didn't I? Now that we are alone and your—ah—young friends are not able to hear me, I must remind you of the serious consequences of engaging in reprisals, Mr Rollison."

Rollison smiled. "I may continue to live in London, I hope."

"If you took my advice, sir, you would leave London for the time being," said Nicholson solemnly. "Those two men who were caught here are on the way to Cannon Row." He hesitated and then asked firmly: "Were they here when I last called?"

"Yes."

"Why didn't you tell me?"

"I didn't think it would help."

"I am an officer of the law, Mr Rollison."

"Oh, yes," said Rollison, "with all the advantages and disadvantages, too. I hoped that I wouldn't have to hand this pair over to you. I thought that if I put the fear of death into them and let them go back to their mob, they would be scared enough to keep the others quiet for a day or two—whereas if they were caught by the police it would spread the conflict immediately. If they believed that I shopped two of their number, I think the leaders of the Slob Mob would be more vengeful than if I let them go."

"I see your point," said Nicholson, still ponderously. "But I warned you in the clearest possible manner that you should not indulge in personal war with these gangsters."

"Yes," Rollison said. "You made your opinion crystal clear."

"Yet you chose to ignore a friendly warning. I came then, as now, without an attendant witness, so that nothing said between us could be used in any formal manner later."

"Yes," said Rollison again. "It was nice of you." He found himself warming towards this man, and yet hesitated to show that too obviously; Nicholson would always want to be taken very seriously. "You know, Inspector, I've played this game for quite a long time, and I might be right occasionally. I think it would have been a mistake to send these chaps to you, and I think you're wrong in advising me not to make a personal issue of it. If this can be confined to a quarrel between me and the Slob Mob, we might get away without serious trouble. If it becomes a clash between the police and the Slob Mob, judging from the mob's present mood I would say that you chaps are going to have your hands full in the East End for weeks. You know as well as I do that when you get gang disorders in the East End, all the other divisions run into trouble—more burglaries and more felonies all the way along. I didn't ignore your advice. I simply decided that it would be a mistake to follow it. I think it's a mistake to have sent those chaps along to Cannon Row, too."

Nicholson looked at him very steadily, appeared to ponder, and then said:

"These men have committed a serious breach of the peace, and in view of what has happened, I must charge them, even if you do not wish to prefer charges. I have no choice."

"That's where I could have helped," Rollison said. "I only have to answer to my conscience. Know what I'm going to do now?"

"I have no idea."

"I am going to see Ginger King and his second-in-command," announced Rollison. "I'm going to tell them that they can bail their two messengers out in the morning. I won't prefer a charge, and you haven't any evidence. The only one you'll be able to charge is the chap caught outside at the back. They might think it's worth sacrificing one Slob for six months or so. I'm sure it's worth trying."

"You mean you will tackle those two men, *alone*?"

"If I go with police protection or any of my friends in

the East End, we'll have a major war on our hands," Rollison said. "Better that I get hurt than a dozen or so do. Sure you won't have that drink?"

Nicholson said, heavily: "I think you're most ill-advised, Mr Rollison, but that doesn't mean that I lack admiration for your courage. Yes, please, I will have a whisky and water, if I may." As Rollison turned to get the drink, he went on: "When will you make this visit, sir?"

"Ah," said Rollison, beaming, "that would be telling. Say when," he added, and began to pour out.

As he did so, he believed that he could read this man's mind on at least one subject: Nicholson was wondering how he could make sure that the intended visit did not take place.

8

JOLLY PLEADS

NICHOLSON went off with his men, after taking statements from the four delegates. Alec Price was still dazed and Rollison suspected that he had slight concussion; certainly he must soon see a doctor. Jonas's knuckles were badly grazed and one finger joint was swollen, although he had managed to protect his face. Doris had a bluish graze on one cheek, and a bruise on her forehead, where she had been roughly handled by her two captors, but she seemed hardly to notice any of these. Only Anne Darby had escaped injury, and Anne did most of the talking, re-iterating what Alec had told the police, emphasising their feeling of guilt when they realised what had happened at the flat.

". . . we wanted to show you we could organise a thing like this without help, that you didn't have to do our thinking for us," Anne said, earnestly, "and we rather took it for granted that no one else would be there. We timed it perfectly—Dorry really did the arranging, didn't you, Doris? We hired some coaches to come and drop us at the end of Gresham Terrace; that was easier than coming in cars, and there would have been the parking problem, too. One or two of the colleges have a brass band, so music was easy. No one expected these—what do you call them?"

"Slobs," put in Doris.

"The Slob Mob," confirmed Rollison.

"Well, no one thought for a moment that they would come," Anne said. "I can't even imagine how they knew what we were going to do. Someone must have told them."

"Did you tell anyone on a newspaper?"

"Well, yes, there's a local Chelham paper—"

"That was enough," Rollison said. "It would be one of the biggest scoops for years." He was not yet fully satisfied that he knew who had tipped off the Slob Mob, but it seemed wise to let the delegates believe that he felt sure. "Well, you made your point all right—a nice, clean job."

"And you're not offended?"

Rollison laughed. "I asked for it!"

"It's damned good of you to take it this way," said Jonas, speaking for the first time since his damaged hands had been dressed; he had four patches of sticking plaster of them. "Mr Roll—" he broke off, as if suddenly tongue-tied.

Doris said for him: "What can we do to make amends, Toff?"

"Make amends for what?"

"Causing you all this trouble."

"Forget it," said Rollison briskly. "You've made your point, haven't you? You can have almost anything you want quoted in the newspapers tomorrow, you'll all be interviewed by the Press. So tell the world what you told me. Point out that this shindy was organised to show the remarkable capability of teenagers. Let your hair down as far as you like."

"And after that?" inquired Doris.

"You'll probably find that your college principals have seen the point," Rollison said.

"We don't mean that," said Doris. "We want to help you with the Slob Mob."

It would have been easy to say that it was the last thing they must do, and even as the girl spoke, Rollison had a mind picture of Nicholson, pontificating on the consequences of such a situation. But if these youngsters were told to do nothing, they would itch to get into the fight. That was the most natural reaction imaginable.

So he laughed.

"What's funny?" Jonas demanded, stung to speech.

Rollison said: "I don't know whether Doris does all

your thinking for you, or whether you all had this in mind,
but before long there'll be quite a job for you to do with
the Slob Mob. Mind if I preach for a minute?"

"You? *Preach?*"

"Don't you ever read the newspapers, Anne?" asked
Doris, sweetly.

Anne was looking at Rollison intently, her blue eyes
bright and enormous.

"I have a queer notion that a lot of the Slobs in the
Mob are what your *bête noires* call good at heart," declared
Rollison. "For everyone who has to be written off as
hopeless, at least one can be—"

"Don't say *saved*," pleaded Doris.

Rollison chuckled again. "Let's say they can be shown
the error of their ways. They can probably be made to
realise that they can have more money in their pockets,
have a far better time, and even help others a bit, if they
don't go around in a slugging gang."

"Until now, I had never met a real optimist," Doris
remarked.

"Mr Rollison, you can't seriously think that those men
who came and attacked us tonight can be—" Anne began.

"Reformed," Doris put in, slyly.

"Some undoubtedly can," declared Rollison firmly.
"I've known the oddest things happen. I even think it
might be possible to reform you four! Now—we ought to
stop talking, and get Alec home, he's not looking so good.
Has any of you a car?"

"No, I'm afraid not," said Anne. "Not here, I mean.
Alec has one, but as I told you, we didn't bring cars today.
We can easily get a taxi, though. Alec's mother will be
frantic when she sees him." She looked sweetly into
Rollison's face, and went on: "Jonas digs with Alec,
though, he can smooth things over. Jonas is an Australian
—did you know?"

"Good-o," said Rollison.

"And Doris and I share a flat," Anne went on. "We
all live within ten minutes walk of each other, so it's no

problem. Mr Rollison, I know I speak for all of us when I say that we'll never forget how you've—you've—"

"Co-operated!" Jonas burst out.

"Jolly," said Rollison, "will you telephone for a taxi?"

* * *

Rollison went down to the street with the four, and was not surprised to find several constables on duty outside, to make sure that the Slob Mob did not attack again to-night. The Chelham delegates scrambled into the taxi, Alec a little more cautiously than the others, for he was still suffering from that blow over the head. Rollison closed the cab door on them, raised a hand, and turned and went back into the house.

When he closed the street door, it was very quiet. He heard music from radios in the other flats, and thought wryly that all of his neighbours had been out, or had kept out of the way. He walked up the stairs slowly. His head was aching, and he found that he had a bruise on his right knee, which made walking slightly painful; a good reason for not hurrying. He let a series of pictures pass through his mind, and no matter how he tried to prevent it, the most vivid one was of Doris Evans with her arms round him, her face upturned, her lips parted in that invitation. He would have to be very careful with Doris, and he did not think that he or anyone else could ever be sure of what was going on in her mind.

He thought that he could assess the others, although it would be easy to make a mistake about them.

They weren't important for the moment, though; but the Slob Mob was. Apart from the fact that he had committed himself with Nicholson, he was quite sure that if he were going to stop this gang trouble from spreading, he would have to see Ginger King and the man Pyne. Nicholson, Jolly, Grice, and nearly everyone else concerned would regard this as an act of folly; but for the time being he did not think that he had any choice.

And as he had said to Jolly, he must not put a foot

wrong. So what should he say, how should he handle the situation when he saw the two Slob leaders? That was the key to success; handling the danger properly.

He let himself into the flat, and found Jolly setting the dining table in the small alcove set aside for this. Jolly made no comment. Rollison went into the bathroom, washed, looked at the scratch, and frowned; it would take several days to heal. The one thing he must not do was to let the Slob Mob think that he was either crying off or pleading for an armistice. He could negotiate only from strength, and with strength, and the truth was that he did not yet know exactly what to do.

It might help if he knew more about Pyne.

It certainly helped that Jolly had prepared a small Aylesbury duck, with orange sauce, and cooked it in a white wine which gave it a flavour which might be expected only from a Paris restaurant; with it, Rollison had a half bottle of Medoc which brought glowing memories of harvest in the vineyards. As if to make sure that he could still triumph under trying conditions, Jolly had made a soufflé so light and so delicately flavoured with lemon that Rollison spent ten minutes relishing it. He declined cheese, but could not resist a cognac. As he cupped the big glass in his hands and sniffed the bouquet, figures seemed to take shape, rising out of the glass. Doris, of course; Anne with her lovely eyes; those six Taggarty girls, dancing willy-nilly along the street, while Lil Ebbutt's Salvation Army lassies watched the Rabelaisian scene with horror. It even brought a smile to his lips at this moment.

He saw an image of Ginger King, and of the man by King's elbow. He did not like what he remembered of this man Harry Pyne.

Then he realised how he must tackle both men.

*   *   *

"Jolly," said Rollison, "I shall be out for at least two hours, and possibly three."

"I see, sir," said Jolly.

"If I'm not back by half past eleven, ask Bill Ebbutt to send a few men to check on the Slob Mob's club house in Whale Street."

"Very good, sir," Jolly said.

"Jolly?"

"Yes, sir?"

"What's got under your skin?"

"I assure you, sir—"

"Jolly," repeated Rollison, firmly, "you may do all kinds of things to me and with me, and I won't complain, but I will not have lies or half lies. What's got under your skin?"

Jolly said: "I think this whole affair is a matter for the police, sir, and that it is folly for you to attempt to deal with it yourself. All the viciousness of these young brutes has revealed itself today, and I think you are quite wrong to take further risks. I thought it was—" he broke off.

"A mistake in the first place?"

"Yes, sir, if you will forgive me for saying so, I did. I couldn't see that the young persons had the slightest justification in coming here on such a pretext."

"And you would have sent them off with a flea in each ear?"

"Metaphorically speaking, no doubt I would, sir."

"Don't you like them?"

"The man Lee and the girl Darby appear to be quite likeable persons, sir. I was unable to come to any conclusion about the boy Price. I am inclined to think that he is mostly a talker."

"Ah."

"Don't you think so, sir?"

"I want to know what you think of Miss Evans?"

"Quite frankly, sir, I don't think I would venture an opinion about that young woman," Jolly said. "In fact I am not at all sure that she does not appear to fit more naturally into the—ah—Slob Mob—than into the other group. I could well be mistaken, but you did ask for my opinion."

"I half share it," Rollison said, thoughtfully. "Right, Jolly. Don't tell the police—at all costs keep them out of the picture unless Ebbutt tells you that they ought to come in. When you talk to Bill, make absolutely sure that he understands that his chaps must keep out of sight, and let me go into the Slob Mob's place by myself. And Jolly."

"Sir?"

"I've been to places like this before."

"And emerged successfully, sir, I know," said Jolly, "but if I may say so, on those occasions there has been a very strong motivation. If one of the young women had been—ah—snatched, I could understand you feeling that you must make this attempt, but I feel so sure that this is essentially a matter for the police. Your pride has been hurt, if I may so venture my opinion, and you may feel that you can only resolve this situation by a personal interview, but I have never known you to act on such a motive before. No one is in danger. There is a very reasonable chance that the Slob Mob will take no further action. The police will patrol their section of the East End very thoroughly, and they will most likely lie low for a while. Quite frankly, sir, I cannot see the slightest justification for any further personal intervention."

After he had stopped, there was silence in the big room, while Rollison looked at his man very straightly, and Jolly's gaze was equally frank.

Then Rollison said: "It's much more than that, Jolly, surely. Much more than a matter of principle, pride, or prejudice. The Slob Mob is keyed up and spoiling for a fight. They may have to sit back for a while because the police are too strong for them, but the police watch will have to relax before long, and the moment it does, the Mob will erupt. They've got to have that fight sooner or later."

Jolly raised his hands, then held them forward in a gesture of appeal, and his voice quivered as he asked:

"But why with *you*, sir?"

"Because I started it," said Rollison simply.

Jolly raised a hand even higher and opened his mouth as if he were going to continue to argue; but he changed his mind, half turned away, and then turned back.

"You will take extreme care, sir, won't you? I have also been involved in such situations for a long time, and my impression of the Slob Mob is most vivid. I think they are very bad indeed. Not only bad, but vicious, savage, and reckless. You will take *extreme* care, won't you?"

"Yes," said Rollison, quietly, "I will indeed."

"Then may I remind you that the two men who came to attack you here carried knives and bicycle chains," said Jolly. "That is the kind of weapon the others are likely to use."

"Probably," agreed Rollison. "But what——?"

Jolly glanced meaningly at the Trophy Wall. Placed on it, and hanging in a small heap on a little shelf, was what looked like a lady's evening handbag, made of a silvery coloured mesh. In fact, it was much larger. Rollison went across, picked it up, and held it against him. It was a link-vest, rather like a cotton cellular garment, soft on the inside, but made of metal on the outside.

Jolly said: "They are most likely to attack the body, sir."

"Yes," agreed Rollison, "they are. And that would blunt a knife point, and make a bicycle chain feel like a feather duster. All right, Jolly, I'll wear it."

"I'm very glad you will," said Jolly.

9

COMPANY

Rollison walked from Gresham Terrace, past the policeman on duty and turned into Piccadilly, where he discovered that a plainclothes man was following him; Jolly was not the only one anxious about what he might do next. He walked briskly, as if out for a late evening stroll, until he came to the traffic lights by the Ritz; then he sprinted across the road against the lights, and as the plainclothes man started to follow, a taxi horn blared out. Rollison nipped down into St James's, and with the detective out of sight, he flagged a taxi.

"Hoylake Garage, near Baker Street," he ordered, and sat back, checked by looking through the rear window that he was not followed and, when he reached the garage in Marylebone Road, stood in a shop doorway for several seconds to make sure that no one had kept up with him. Satisfied, he went into the garage, which operated an all night mechanical and petrol service, and which also hired out cars. Rollison was known here as a regular customer, and this evening he selected a black $2\frac{1}{2}$ litre Jaguar which had all the speed he was likely to want. He drove out of the garage, checked again that no one was following him, and set out for the East End. The weight of the chain vest was spread so evenly that it did not trouble him, and in no way did it restrict his freedom of movement.

Once he was in Holborn, traffic dropped away, and the City streets were almost deserted. He turned into Aldgate and went past the station, then slowed down. He was five minutes' drive away from the old club where the Slob Mob foregathered, and he was quite sure that near Aldgate station and Whitechapel the Mob would have its runners, to report on any development which looked interesting—such as more police cars than usual, or the movements of the Taggarty Gang, or even the movements of the Toff. Rollison knew that he was recognised by most of the men in sight, and had no doubt at all that the news of his arrival was going ahead of him.

He drove slowly.

It would not greatly surprise him if there was a rush at the car from a side street; or if one of the Mob drove another car out of a side street at him, set on causing an accident. He was prepared for either emergency, and was very watchful, but nothing happened even when he turned out of the wide, well-lit streets into the long, narrow turnings which led towards the river and the docks. Here the tiny houses were built close together, like rows of decaying teeth, grim, drab, grey, ill-lit. A few people were about and, one of the most remarkable indications of change in social habits since the Toff had first roamed London, a car was parked outside one of the mean little houses every thirty or forty yards or so. He saw several pairs of policemen in uniform strolling about, and they would probably recognise him. The fact that the police were out in strength might account for the fact that he had not been given too warm a welcome.

He turned into Whale Street.

At the end of this street was the Slob Mob's headquarters and these had been selected long ago in the time of a good leader.

Members paid a subscription, often forced out of them by Pyne, to meet the general expenses of rent, lighting, heating and even a telephone. The old club house, years ago a Civil Defence Post, later rented by a combined church organisation as the Youth Club, was built at one end of a small warehouse, which had not been used for years. The upper part of the main building was utterly derelict, the floorboards were rotting, the roof was full of small holes so that rain leaked through; but the Mob's headquarters were on the ground floor, where the floors had been repaired. There was reasonably good furniture, and one big room had ample space for dancing.

Still registered as a club, there was a dancing and music licence, and an old grand piano; there was even a stage.

Lights blazed from windows on either side of the front door, which had a porch rather like the entrance to a church. There was ample room for parking close to the club, but Rollison did not turn into the parking area; he reversed into an alley, and left the car so that he could drive off quickly. On the other side of the club was a narrow road, a cul-de-sac, which led to the back, or the stage, door. Cars were parked along here, too, quite close together. Slob Mob members ran to old new-looking motor-scooters, battered looking small cars; most of the engines were undoubtedly hotted up.

The Mob knew he was here, of course; if they decided to stop him, they would soon do damage to his car, Rollison knew. He relied on one human factor which Jolly would say did not exist; arousing the better nature as well as the curiosity of Ginger King, of Harry Pyne, and of the Mob's members. They would be eager to know why the Toff had ventured into their territory and what he wanted; they might even believe that he had come to make terms.

A shadowy figure moved out of a doorway in one of the houses leading away from the Club. Rollison was aware of that, but took no notice. Another shadowy figure darted into sight for a moment, and dived into the porch and doorway; warning of his arrival was being taken to the leaders. Rollison walked along briskly, seeing no one on either side of him but aware that he was followed. He reached the Club doorway. No one was in sight. He turned to look behind him, and caught a glimpse of a girl's figure outlined against a street lamp. He could not see who she was, she was too far away. He waited. The girl walked briskly towards him, but then stopped at the corner of the alley where he had parked the car. He wished that she would come closer and pass beneath another street lamp, but she did not, and he still did not know who it was. Remembering what had happened to the Taggarty Mob's girls, it would be surprising if any of the Slob girls were to be on her own.

It was surprising that any girl ventured out quite alone in this danger spot, too. There was always a risk that some of the Slobs would come and have their fun. The girl hesitated, then disappeared into the alley; to Rollison that seemed even more remarkable, for the alley was narrow and dark, and as he had passed he had seen that even the one gas lamp fastened to a wall bracket was turned very low. He listened for the return of her footsteps, but did not hear them; so she had stopped walking. Was she in his car? He had not locked it—a locked door invited damage and destruction where the Slob Mob was concerned. He wished he hadn't seen her, because she was taking his mind off the main job, which lay beyond these doors.

She might have gone to meet a boy friend, of course.

Rollison turned his back on the corner and the car, and stepped into the porch. Floorboards creaked. Light blazed out from a fanlight above his head, and there was a streak of light running from the top to the bottom of the door, in the middle. He tried a handle, and pushed it down; no one moved inside, but he felt quite sure that there would be a reception party. He could almost hear Jolly's voice and see Jolly's gloom: Jolly was so sure that he was making a mistake.

Was it a mistake?

Who was that girl, and what had happened to her?

Rollison pushed the right-hand side of the door open, and then dodged to one side; but nothing happened. He stopped it from swinging to, and went into a wide hall, with brown linoleum on the floor, walls painted a bright red on one side and a bright green on the other. The sound of music came clearly, but no other sounds. On the right was a door marked: *This is it*, and had a crude drawing of a girl's face on it; on the other side was a much simpler: *Men*. The only other doorway out of this hall seemed to lead to a staircase, and he stepped to it and looked up the uncarpeted stairs. No one was there. Had he not known better he would have thought that he had managed to get in unobserved.

Ahead were more double doors leading to the main room.

He stepped to these, glancing behind him to the right and the left, but no one appeared.

He put a hand on each of the double doors, and pushed simultaneously and stepped inside.

As he appeared, thirty or forty couples on the floor seemed to be shocked into sudden movement; one moment they had been dancing a slow fox trot, the next they swung into a wild orgy of rock and roll. A pianist, sax player, and a man at the drums started to play with a frenzy which told Rollison that it had all been laid on, that this was exactly the kind of reception they planned.

No one took the slightest notice of him.

He did not think that he had ever been ignored like this in the East End before. In a way, he was glad, for it gave him time to take in the fantastic sight of massed Teddy Boys and their girls. Every boy seemed to be wearing a curly, oiled wig, thick-soled shoes padded the floor, shoulders swayed up and down inside jackets padded to giant size.

The whirling, jumping, swaying, swinging dancers pretended to be oblivious of Rollison. The music seemed to be stepped up to a swifter, zany rhythm. A few couples sitting at tables round the walls were beating time with glasses, feet or hands, making a raucous din, and not a single person appeared to be looking at Rollison.

It was very well done indeed.

He had the same feeling that he had known after realising that the Slob Mob was attacking the flat at Gresham Terrace; a feeling of disquiet in case he had under-rated them, and that there might be a clever guiding intelligence. He wished he could see Ginger, but could not pick him out, nor did he see the man with the long narrow face. They were probably keeping out of sight deliberately. He stood watching the frenzied mob, and noticed that one or two of the girls and several of the men glanced at him, although they glanced as quickly away. A tallish youth with a mob of frizzy hair was dancing with a diminutive Chinese girl, he was slinging her over his shoulder, between his legs, giving a savage, acrobatic performance, and the girl was smiling a set and glassy smile all the time. Others were nearly as abandoned. The band was beating louder and to a fast, faster rhythm—and still no one took the slightest notice of the visitor. Rollison had no doubt at all that this was a matter of cleverly applied tactics; they were set on making him feel small; the leaders were showing the ordinary members of the gang just how insignificant the Toff was compared with them. Without a word being spoken, without a gesture, without even acknowledging his presence, they were making a fool of him.

Yes, it was tortuously clever.

He began to smile; the many quick glances sent his way called for nonchalance. He pushed his light-weight trilby to the back of his head at a rakish angle. He took out a cigarette, and thrust it into a short cigarette holder, then lit it. He surveyed the whole crowd while the frenzy grew greater, and told himself that when they stopped even these youngsters would be on the point of exhaustion, the tempo was so wild.

The music stopped.

On the instant, the dancers stopped too, only a few flurries of movement followed the last boom on the drum; there was no doubt at all that this had been pre-arranged —none that the Slob Mob took a pride in its dancing, either. No one stared at Rollison, only at other dancers. He wondered what would happen if he turned his back on them, and felt quite sure that they would be transformed into a howling mob, intent on beating him up. He did not move for at least two minutes, but they were equally still; they meant to make him break the stillness and the silence.

He stepped towards the little Chinese girl, who was facing him, and could not easily look away. He brushed against another girl whose skirt was above her knees, and whose jumper was stretched so tight that in silhouette she must appear to be naked. He stepped past the man who had been dancing with the Chinese girl, without touching him; if he touched a man or trod on his toes or dug him with his elbow, it might be the signal for attack. He stood in front of the Chinese girl, and said in a clear voice which would have been familiar in any Mayfair *salon*:

"You were quite wonderful. Would you care to dance?"

Her eyes seemed very narrow, almond shaped, and the colour was of honey brown. Her eyebrows were dark and smooth, and she had a perfect complexion, reminding Rollison of Anne Darby. He held his arms out towards her, and she did not know what to do. He moved still further forward, took her right hand in his left, slid his right hand round her waist, and began to dance to the tune of an imaginary quick step; a brisk tempo, but not wild like the rock and roll. After the first moment of surprise and awkwardness, the Chinese girl fell into step, and Rollison felt her body swaying to that imagined rhythm, and could understand how the magic of the dancing got into her body.

Her partner could make trouble, though; any of the others could make trouble. But it seemed certain to Rollison that if there was a really clever directing intelligence here, then a different approach would be made.

He didn't yet know what was likely to follow, could not even be sure that he was right, but at least the first reaction was good. The girl's partner made no attempt to stop him, and other couples moved aside to let him glide past. He was smiling at his partner, and began to talk lightly and inconsequentially, still using the voice which must sound almost foreign to the ears of these youngsters.

Youngsters, as they looked? Or young devils, as they had behaved that afternoon?

He saw three youths whom he recognised, and then caught sight of Ginger King, a raven-haired, bosomy girl with a too-tight, shiny dress, Harry Pyne, and a curiously flat-chested and studious-looking girl. All of these were at a corner table raised slightly above the rest, so that they could get a good view of everything that was going on. Ginger King was looking at Pyne, as if wanting to know what he should do next.

10

DANCE, DUDE, DANCE

This was the first time that Rollison had seen either man at close quarters. If Ginger King had been somewhere else, with a normal crowd, for instance, he would have seemed pleasant enough. There was an unexpectedly good-natured look about him, while his expression of uncertainty made him look very young. But no one was likely to find anything attractive about the man Pyne. There was an indefinable expression in his eyes, a twist to his thin lips, a cast to his whole countenance, which warned Rollison that he would have to be very, very careful with this man. Lombroso's theory might have been disproved long ago, but in Rollison's experience it was still possible to tell the really bad from the half-and-half; and he thought that this man had the appearance of the man with evil born in him.

He said clearly: "On the whole I prefer dancing to music, don't you?"

"Yes, I do," the girl said, speaking for the first time in a rich nasal Cockney, which nearly sounded like: "*Yeh, Oi dow.*" She had never yet seen China. The words were certainly loud enough to carry to the ears of the two leaders. Rollison made no attempt to look over his shoulder, but as he turned round her saw Pyne's eyes light up, and knew that this was the moment of decision. Pyne leaned forward to Ginger King. King's face was suddenly split in two with a grin, and he raised his hand and waved it. After a split second's pause, there was a bang on the drums, then the pianist began to play a quickstep. Rollison felt the girl's movements quicken, knew that music put some kind of magic in her. Ginger stood up and waved, and suddenly every one began to dance to the same tune, but after a few seconds it became faster; too fast for a quickstep, fast enough for a zamba. Rollison changed step. The girl followed as if she knew automatically what to do. The music grew louder and the rhythm faster, wild frenzy took possession of the Slob Mob again. Ginger King dragged his bosomy beauty into the crowd, and danced as if he were made for rhythm, leaving Pyne and the studious-looking girl at the table. Pyne was tapping the table with his fingers to the speed of the rhythm. Rollison saw a man go over to him, and whisper. Pyne looked startled, paused, and then stood up. Without a word to the girl, he strolled across the room to a door in the corner, and went out. No one appeared to notice that he had gone.

The band swung into a calypso. The tiny girl in Rollison's arms seemed to accept the challenge of the dance, seemed to defy her partner to keep pace with her, was surprised at first and then delighted when he swung into the step without the slightest hesitation. But for the fact that Pyne had gone out, obviously surprised by some news, Rollison would have felt that he was on top of the situation, but now he kept wondering what was going on. He watched the doors at every opportunity, but no one appeared.

The rhythm grew faster, it was inevitable that they should swing into a rock and roll tune, inevitable that the crowd near Rollison and the Chinese girl should give them good room to move. Everyone was watching Rollison and the girl, everyone knew by now what Ginger King was up to—he was making Rollison dance, to show him how out-classed he was; the band was going to keep this tempo up until he had to stop from exhaustion. It was a clever move, and had the touch which he had already recognised in the activities of the Slob Mob. They would take it for granted that a man in his early forties could not stand the pace, and as he danced with the 'Chinese' girl it dawned on him that most of those present regarded him as old; as the four delegates had.

There were things they didn't know, however; that he

kept as fit as any man in London, that his body was as
lithe and supple as any youngster's, that he knew every
hold in wrestling and in Judo, and that there was hardly a
trick on the dance floor that he hadn't tried, even if he
hadn't practised many of them for a long time. He jigged
back from the girl, and she did a crazy half circle about
him. He slid his arm out of the right sleeve of his coat,
held it to him, and then joined the girl again; now all the
others were watching more intently. He kept glancing at
the doors, but there was no sign at all of Harry Pyne.

Had Pyne gone to pull off some vicious trick?

The girl swayed away from him again, and it seemed to
Rollison that she was almost in a trance. Her eyes were
rolling, her teeth were showing, beautifully white, and she
moved with frenzied rhythm. Rollison slid his other arm
free, and held the coat out towards a dancer near him.
The impudence of the gesture succeeded; the boy took
it. "Thanks," said Rollison. He was already too warm,
the room was very hot. For the first time he wished that
he hadn't been persuaded to wear the chain vest; it was
far, far warmer than wool.

The girl came swaying towards him, head jerked to the
right, head jerked to the left, right side thrust forward,
hand outstretched, left side thrust forward, hand outstretched; it was all mechanical and her first partner
would have seized her wrist and flung her over his
shoulder, or between his legs. Rollison let her go. Still
in that trance, she swayed and bobbed about and round
him, and then thrust her hand towards him again. This
time Rollison took her wrist, placed a hand at her waist,
and tossed her upwards. The light, lithe body seemed to
float off the floor, over his shoulder, and to land with unexpected gentleness behind him as he swung round. A
little gasp went up. The girl looked delighted as she swayed
again, her other side and hand towards him now; and he
repeated the manoeuvre.

"*Ooooh,*" seemed to rise from the crowd as a long sigh.
Rollison thought: 'I wonder how long they'll keep it

up'. He knew one answer, of course—until they were sure that he would collapse from exhaustion. Now that the first exhilaration had worn off, he began to wonder how long he could keep going at the pace, for the rhythm was getting faster, many of the other dancers were concentrating on what they were doing, and paying him little attention. Studying the little Chinese creature in front of him, it was easy to believe that she was about to swoon. Rollison was feeling not only hot but sticky, and it was small consolation to see that several of the others were, too, and that there was a film of perspiration on his partner's forehead. The pace was so fierce that he almost forgot the fact that Pyne had gone out, but now and again he glanced at the table where Pyne and Ginger King had been. He saw Ginger walking towards it, mopping his forehead; half-a-dozen other couples had given up, too. This was a pace which very few of them had danced to before, the pace deliberately set to kill the Toff.

Then, he saw Pyne.

He did not like what he saw, for the youth stood with one hand in his pocket, the other just in front of him, singling him out for attention. He was alone, and he was smiling. The smile was not at all good to see. Rollison had never been so sure that a man was bad, or that he was gloating. What had happened, what gave him such satisfaction? Was the moment of climax almost here?

Now that he was almost on the point of exhaustion, was Pyne going to strike? That was what it looked like—and it seemed as if Rollison's effort was doomed to fail, as if Jolly had been far more right than he.

More couples dropped out, but the rhythm became even faster, without a moment's let-up. The Chinese girl continued to dance as if in a trance, there was savagery in the very movements, in the speed—a savagery which reminded him of some of the wild tribal dances of Africa, a kind of drunken, orgiastic fury. He knew that his one hope of easement was that the Chinese girl might give up.

He did not think that likely.

He was a bloody fool ever to think that a man of his age would compete with the best of these youths—and the fact that no more than a dozen people were left on the floor was really no consolation. Unless he outlasted them all the effort would be wasted. Pyne knew that, of course —perhaps he had simply come to gloat.

Pyne moved towards Ginger King, who looked as if he was gasping for breath from his exertions; King wasn't in good condition. Rollison felt his own chest tightening, as if a steel band were round it, and someone was closing the band with a lever; it became harder and harder to bear the tightness which grew into pain. He felt the breath rasping through his nostrils, and knew that he was a fool to try to carry on. It was the uncertainty about Pyne which kept him going, now; the way Pyne stared with such gloating insolence—and the way Ginger King started when Pyne spoke to him, then looked towards the stage, then back at Rollison.

The stage? Were they going to make him do a solo dance up there? It would be a smart move; it would make him a laughing stock, and from the beginning that was what they had set out to do.

Then unbelievingly, he felt the girl sag in his arms. Her half-closed eyes were glazed. He knew that she was almost at the point of exhaustion, her legs wouldn't carry her much longer. That gave him one good moment, pouring new hope into him, and he pulled her towards him again, feeling the flatness of her body, the dead weight of her resistance.

Next, he saw a girl pushed on to the stage, spinning round and round, and a sheet or blanket fell away.

She was dressed in bra and panties. She had a figure in a thousand. She walked with a curious mixture of hesitancy and boldness, and kept glancing over her shoulder as if afraid of what she could see there.

She was Doris Evans.

*　　　*　　　*

Rollison recognised her on the instant; and at the same moment realised who had been in Whale Street, and gone into that alley. This lunatic of a girl had come here, had expected him, waited for him—and had been caught by the Slob Mob. If she had given him a moment's warning, if she had even hinted that she would come here, he could have stopped her.

That was why she hadn't told him in advance.

Now she stood at the centre of the empty stage. He could see the crowd looking away from him and the Chinese girl toward Doris. He could not see but he could imagine the Slob members in the wings—they had driven her out there, of course, on Harry Pyne's orders, and the problem now was to know what they would make her do next.

Strip tease even further?

Rollison could not be sure, could only be sure that it would be something to taunt him, something to make him lose his self-control. The opportunity for Harry Pyne would be far too great to miss.

Then the Chinese girl seemed to fold up.

Rollison prevented her from falling, and held her loosely. As he did so, the music stopped; all the timing here was perfect. He drew the girl closer to him, then held her firmly. The blood was pounding through his ears, his head was going round and round, he doubted whether he could take a straight course to the stage; but he had to keep his feet, while every second he gained would be invaluable. As the seconds ticked by and the Mob looked from him to Doris, and then back to him, he heard a few laughs, a few titters. No one was really near him. He stood with the sweat dripping down his face, the perspiration soaking his vest and shirt, his muscles quivering from the reaction.

They were just waiting for him; Pyne believed in using his time to the fullest advantage. But he was giving Rollison time; a minute, two minutes, three minutes, while his breathing became quieter and the sweat seemed to drip from every pore, but his muscles were a little less quivery, and he could move forward. He hitched the girl higher in front of him and began to move forward; that was what Pyne wanted of course, to make him move, but Pyne's cat-and-mouse methods could cut two ways. Everyone here, including Pyne himself, was wondering what Rollison would do next.

He took long, slow strides. He was aware of Doris staring at him, and he could believe that she was regretting all she had done, and must wish herself a thousand miles away from here. The table where Ginger and Pyne and their girls had been was near the side of the stage, and Rollison turned towards it. He was smiling a set smile, but every step and every second gave him more confidence and more strength, and again he realised exactly what he had to do.

He reached the table. He was within a few feet of Ginger, and ever closer to Pyne, whose eyes were narrowed and very black; who did not quite know what to do, and for the moment had to leave the initiative with the Toff.

Rollison put the Chinese girl on to a chair, lowering her gently, making her comfortable before straightening up, and pushing his fingers through his hair. Then he stared up at Doris, grinned, and said:

"Care to dance, Dorry?"

After a startled pause, Ginger echoed gustily: "Care to *dance*. You hear that?"

Two or three others echoed: "*Dance?*"

One girl said: "*Boy, has he got what it takes!*"

Rollison turned away from Ginger King and Harry Pyne. There were five wooden steps leading to the stage itself, and he climbed up them, still moving slowly, giving himself every possible moment of respite. He did not know what to do next; he could not be sure how long he could keep on dancing, and he knew only that he had to get up there and do something to protect the girl. Later he could tell her exactly what he thought of her for this crazy thing. As he pushed a curtain aside he saw three of the Mob standing in the wings. Doris's clothes were strewn about, the trio seemed to be smiling very tensely, as if they felt something of the uncertainty of the situation, too. One of them carried a billiards cue, and obviously he held it so as to prod Doris and make her go where he wanted.

Rollison moved towards Doris, who crossed her bosom with her arms in unexpected shyness. Then he saw that she was not looking at him, but at one of the men on the dance floor. Rollison reached her side, and turned round —and saw that she was staring at Ginger King. Ginger was standing absolutely still, and gaping. The bosomy girl by his side was scowling, and Pyne's girl was watching intently. The little Chinese had not moved from the chair where Rollison had left her.

Ginger relaxed, gave that broad grin again, and in a fair imitation of Rollison's voice, he called:

"Would you care to *dawnce*, chicken?" He leapt for the platform, landed lightly, and ran towards Doris with his arms outstretched. He shot Rollison a casual glance, and jerked his thumb towards the wings, obviously an order to leave.

At least this would give Rollison a further respite; but it would not solve the problem of how to get Doris away from here. He could see that Pyne was no more pleased than Ginger's girl friend, but the situation was out of their hands. Another crisis would build up soon, and Pyne would almost certainly cause it, but that didn't matter for the moment. The band started to play again, this time a quick-step. Ginger slid his arms round Doris—and then Rollison, glancing towards the wings where the three youths stood, saw the electric switches on the wall behind the curtain.

11

DARKNESS

ROLLISON watched as Ginger swung Doris round, and
noticed the way Doris began to dance in rhythm, as if
dancing was in her blood, too. She was still badly
scared, but no one could question her courage. She
looked over Ginger's shoulder at the Toff, who winked;
he was sure that no one else could see the wink. Down on
the main floor most of the couples were dancing again, but
Harry Pyne was standing and staring at Ginger, as if his
puppet had become a creature he didn't understand.
Rollison stood watching the dancers until the man with
the billiard cue realised that he was serving no useful
purpose; he moved out of the wings and jumped down.
The other two followed suit, and it was remarkable that
no one here now seemed to think that there was the
slightest danger from Rollison—except Pyne, who was
watching him closely.

Rollison felt almost himself again. There was weakness
in his leg and arm muscles, and he was going to be very
stiff in the morning, but at least he would be able to put
up a fight now—if he had to. He did not think that Pyne
would allow the initiative to be out of his hands for long.
Pyne stood watching the couple. They danced very well,
and Doris's long, slim legs were quite beautiful. Her near-
nakedness was more apparent because her captors had
allowed her to wear her shoes. She had a slim waist,
beautifully curved, and quite lovely shoulders. As she
turned round in the dance, she looked questioningly,
pleadingly at Rollison, and he gave a little jerk of his head,
hoping that Pyne could not see it. She did not seem to
understand. He backed further towards the lighting
panel, and as she drew nearer again, pointed to it; he saw
from the gleam in her eyes that she grasped what he meant.

Ginger swung her round in another circle, and Rollison saw that her body was going more tense, she actually missed a step.

Pyne whispered something to his girl friend, while the girl whom Ginger had neglected was sitting and glowering. Then Pyne moved towards the wooden steps—and Rollison put out his right hand and pressed down the switches, all eight of them. Seven lights went out at once; the eighth took a split second longer. The first reaction was of utter silence, almost a deathly hush. Then Rollison heard a thudding sound; someone had fallen over on the stage. He heard sharp footsteps, followed by a gasp, before something went flying over the boards and struck his foot. Next moment, soft warm flesh was quivering close to him, Doris was almost in his arms.

"I tripped him up," she gasped. "Don't let him catch me."

Now men were shouting, girls screaming, someone flashed on a torch. The odds against getting away through the hall were hideous, but Rollison swung round, with Doris, towards the door which led from the wings. He heard more thumping of footsteps, then the clatter of metal; chairs or tables were being thrown at the stage. A light glowed against a window, outside, and he could just make out the shape of a door.

"He's going out the back. Stop him!" shouted Pyne. "Get a move on, you ——"

Rollison reached the door. He could not make out the shape of the handle but guessed where it was, and touched and clutched a round metal knob. If the bolts were home, he would probably have no time at all. He pulled, and the door banged back against his foot. Light from a street gas lamp glowed yellow. Doris fell against him, and he heard her gasp as with pain, and realised that she had stubbed her toes. Before that ordeal by dancing he would have been able to carry her with ease; now he wondered whether he would be able to take her far; but he had to try. He could just discern her figure. He bent a little, slid one arm round her shoulders and one beneath her knees, and hoisted her from the ground. He could feel her breath, then her hair, on his cheeks, but she didn't speak. She was breathing very hard, as if quite terrified. Several cars were beneath the street lamp. Even if he could get into one it would take too long to start the engine and drive off; in a moment the Slob Mob would be swarming out of the front doors and rushing this way. The truth was that he wouldn't have a chance.

Then he heard a man shout in a high-pitched voice:

"*There they are!*"

For a moment he thought that it was one of the Slob Mob, but suddenly realised how wrong he was. Torch lights flashed on, headlamps blazed out from cars at the far end of the street and against them he could see dozens of weaving bodies, among them Jonas Lee.

He thought he heard Jonas whoop, as if with joy.

A police whistle sounded in the distance, and Rollison knew that the police had discovered that a gang fight was in the making, and were sending for reinforcements. This was no time to think, to worry or to fear. He had only to protect Doris for another five minutes; it might not be necessary even for as long as that. He reached one of the parked cars, opened the door with his right hand, and let Doris slide to the ground.

"Get inside and wait for the police," he ordered. "I'll see you're all right until they come." He helped her in, hand stroking her chilling flesh in an accidental caress, and then saw her, just a vague white blur crouched in the little car. He felt a moment of satisfaction, almost of triumph— until he heard a man speak from the pavement just behind him; a man whom he had neither seen nor heard.

The man said: "I'm going to kill you, Toff."

*　　*　　*

That was Harry Pyne.

Rollison was standing against the car door, twisting round. He could just make out Pyne; the man had crept up behind the other cars when Rollison had been too busy to keep watch behind. He must have stepped without making a sound across the cobbles, and now stood there, completely sure of himself. In the distance police whistles shrilled, and nearer at hand was the thudding, thumping, gasping, and swearing of fighting men; occasionally there came a little squeal of pain.

"Don't make any mistake," Pyne went on. "I'm going to kill you."

He was sure to have a knife.

Rollison turned slowly on his heels so that he wasn't at such a disadvantage, and saw the shimmering streak of steel close to Pyne's waist. He heard a shuffle of movement nearby and knew that others were coming to support Pyne. He expected the other to leap forward, and to stab him, at any moment, but Pyne was crouching, still biding his time. A beam of light shot out, touched the corner of the car, touched the Toff's head, and then kept nearly still. Rollison dodged to one side.

Steel went *clang!* against the metal of the car.

"I'm going to kill you, Toff," Harry Pyne repeated.

The light was still shining on Rollison, and he could not get away from it. It shone in his eyes, dazzling him; as it was meant to. He screwed up his eyes and stared across the narrow street towards Pyne, but could not make out the man's figure, could not be sure how near or how far away he was. He was gasping for breath. If Pyne leapt forward there would at least be a chance, but Pyne was taking his time; that was the man's great characteristic and his weakness; he loved to have time to gloat over his victim. A second torch beam shone into Rollison's eyes, they were keeping his face in the focus of the light—as they would keep an aircraft in the beams of searchlights.

"Good-bye, Toff," Pyne sneered.

Rollison bent his knees and dropped forward, hands thrust out, and for a moment he vanished from the light. He heard a rustle of sound, a *hisssss* as a knife sliced towards him, and he gritted his teeth. Pyne had anticipated his move, and aimed low.

Rollison felt the heavy impact of the knife on his back, beautifully judged—but for the chain vest, it would have gone between his ribs. The blow hurt; but the knife fell. He heard Pyne swear, saw the light snake downwards, and saw a pair of shiny shoes—Pyne's. He flung himself forward, hands outstretched for the other's ankles, and as he fell, he twisted his body to one side. He sensed rather than saw the sweeping movements of Pyne's arm, actually saw the blade of another knife, the hand gripping it and the gold of Pyne's cuff-link, vivid in a snaking beam of torch-light. But Pyne had made his big mistake by being over-confident, and assuming that the thrown knife would do all he wanted of it. The impetus of the slashing follow-up carried him forward, off his balance.

Rollison gripped his ankles, and tugged savagely. He heard Pyne swear, then heard the knife clatter to the cobbles, and felt Pyne kicking out desperately, suddenly in fear. He freed one ankle. The toe of the shoe caught Rollison on the side of the head, but the blow wasn't hard enough to hurt. Pyne crashed down. Lights weaved and waved, faces, shoes, clothes, cobbles all seemed to show up vividly in the silvery light. Rollison rolled over and over, and then heard the sounds which for a few seconds he had almost forgotten: the thudding, gasping, and squealing of the fighters, the roar of car engines, the high-pitched scream of police whistles.

Then came a tremendous bellow in a voice which he just recognised.

"Cut and run, Slobs! Cut and run!"

That was Ginger King, acting as leader in his own right, and doing the only wise thing. Rollison was close against a car, lying full length. The torch lights went out, but there was reflected light from the distant car head-lamps. He saw Pyne scrambling to his feet, and other men running. He could not be sure that the danger was over for him, yet—but suddenly Pyne and the others turned and ran towards the back of the club house. Rollison heard a door slam a moment later, and realised that they thought the best way of escape was on the other side.

Then, he heard Doris Evans ask anxiously: "Are you all right, Toff? Are you all right?"

He eased himself over to one side, so that he could look towards the car from which she was speaking. He could just make out her face, against the open window of the car; and as he did so, the door opened and she stepped out, unbelievably white and virginal-looking. She rushed towards him, as if driven by a great anxiety. "Toff! Are you—"

"If I were you, I'd run back to the stage and put some clothes on," said Rollison. "The police might not think much of you if they see you as a strip-tease act. The Slobs won't be there now, they're too scared of the police, so you go first. I'll come in a jiffy."

She hesitated.

"Today," Rollison urged.

She bent over him, put her arm round his waist, and helped him to his feet; she had quite remarkable strength for a girl. Only when he was standing upright did she turn and run towards the stage door. The sound of the fighting had died away, no police whistles sounded, but there was a great deal of scraping of feet, subdued voices, now and again a "*No, you don't.*" He swayed, and knew that he was nearly out on his feet. The only wise course now was to say nothing; watch out for more trouble from Pyne, but say nothing to the police. He made himself step towards the stage door. It was open. Lights were on above the stage, and he saw Doris stepping into a skirt, and pulling it up briskly; she already had on a jumper. She saw him, and her face lit up. Then a deep voice spoke from the back of the room, out of Rollison's sight.

"Keep still, all of you."

Doris shrugged herself into her coat, and then thrust her hand out to Rollison, holding a wispy thing that looked too small to be a suspender belt, but was. She also held a pair of crumpled stockings.

"Stuff those in your trouser pockets!" she whispered.

"*Keep still there!*" bellowed the man out of sight, and came thumping towards the stage with at least three other policemen behind him. A table overturned. Two men jumped up on to the stage and Rollison and Doris turned towards them. Two others reached the wings.

"Hallo," Rollison welcomed them, cheerfully. "Thank you for coming. How big were the ones that got away?"

A uniformed sergeant said: "Mr *Rol*lison!"

"And this is Miss Evans," said Rollison, gravely. "Did anyone happen to see my jacket? It was very hot when I first came in."

*　　*　　*

He found his jacket, slung over the back of a wooden chair. Dotted about the tables, the floor, and the chairs were girls' handbags, compacts, cigarette cases, packets of cigarettes, matches, handkerchiefs and bottles, mostly of innocuous soft drinks. The floor near the tables was littered with cigarette butts. The heavy tread of the police echoed loudly about the club, and police poked in every odd corner for the odd Slob who might have stayed behind. Outside, one Black Maria held seven girls and three boys, all of them young and some fringe members of the Mob, all a little scared. Most of these were Jonas Lee's friends, but Jonas and most of the others, as well as nearly all of the Slob Mob, had heard the police whistles in time to get away.

One thing really puzzled Rollison; the speed with which Pyne and the men with him had disappeared. They had gone into the side entrance, but obviously had not gone out at the front; the police had been in strength there. This meant that there was a secret way out—or, at least, a way not known to the police, otherwise it would have been blocked. Was it an old Civil Defence exit?

That way out was worth finding.

But Rollison's immediate problem was to explain his

presence and Doris's to the police. His own would have been difficult enough. He was reassuring himself that at least he would have to deal with an East End Divisional officer whom he knew, when Detective Inspector Nicholson stalked into the club.

12

THE LADY LIES

THERE was a lot of quality in Nicholson, and a great deal of authority, too. As he came in, Rollison had an impression of a man with an irresistible plodding strength, of great stubbornness, and also of quiet anger. It was strange that after so few meetings, Nicholson could be so impressive, and it dawned on Rollison as he watched the man that in the years ahead Nicholson could become one of the big names at the Yard. There was no glint of recognition and certainly none of friendliness in his manner, and he looked at Rollison in exactly the same way as he looked at Doris—and as he would at any prisoners.

He stopped at the stage and stared up at Rollison and yet somehow managed not to be at a disadvantage.

"I would like your explanation of this at once, Mr Rollison," he said.

"You could give me time to get my breath back," Rollison retorted.

"There is no time to spare. A second unlawful gathering has taken place tonight and a serious gang battle with grievous loss of life has been narrowly averted. What do you know of it?"

Rollison said: "I came—"

"He came because I'd made a fool of myself, and was desperate for help," Doris Evans interrupted quickly, and she made Nicholson look at her in surprise. "I thought I could be clever and I came out here to try to talk to Ginger King."

"You did *what*?"

"I came to talk to Ginger," said Doris. She raised her head defiantly, as if shocked to think that Nicholson might doubt her word. "I rather liked what I saw of him this evening, and I thought it was sheer lunacy for people

97

like us to be fighting. I thought I might be able to reason
with him, but I was so scared when I got here, because
men started to follow me. I got to a telephone and called
Mr Rollison, and he rushed here at once. I—I was being
held a prisoner when he arrived. But for him I don't
know what would have happened."

"I *see*," said Nicholson. He eyed the girl steadily and
thoughtfully, as if trying to make up his mind whether to
believe her or not. He turned to Rollison, who expected
to be reminded that he had told the police where he was
coming, but instead Nicholson inquired:

"What time did this call come, Mr Rollison?"

Rollison answered: "Soon after eight-thirty, I suppose.
I'd just finished dinner."

"I *see*," said Nicholson again, and breathed down his
nose. "Who were the persons who kidnapped you, Miss
Evans?"

"It was dark, I didn't see them clearly."

"Would you be able to recognise them or—"

"I've told you, I didn't see them clearly!"

"I was about to ask," went on Nicholson, as steadfast as
any steamroller, "would you be able to recognise any of
the men whom you saw here and who held you against
your will?"

"Well—not for certain," Doris said.

"That is unfortunate." Nicholson paused. "Mr.
Rollison, what is your account of what took place?"

Rollison said: "I came, I danced, they tried to show me
how worn out and senile I am, but it didn't work out
quite the way they expected. As soon as I thought there
was a chance to get Doris away, I doused the lights. I
didn't know that she had been followed by her friends."

"Were you aware of that?" inquired Nicholson, this
time of Doris.

"No," she answered promptly. "They must have discovered where I was coming, and followed. I wish they
hadn't. It was bad enough before, and it's far worse
now."

"I am glad you at least appreciate that," said Nicholson heavily. "What organisation do your friends belong to?"

"No actual organisation," Doris replied. "We used to belong to different Student Societies, but we didn't get a kick out of them, and—"

"So you think you can get a thrill out of promoting rivalry with a rival gang in a different part of London," Nicholson said heavily. "Miss Evans, I must ask you to come with me to the Divisional Headquarters for questioning. I am not sure that you yet fully appreciate the seriousness of what you are doing. Mr Rollison, I am sure that you do fully appreciate the seriousness and in this instance it appears that you had some justification for coming here, but you omitted one obligatory duty."

"What was that?" asked Rollison.

"You omitted to inform the police immediately of the precarious situation in which Miss Evans reported that she found herself. You should have realised that the police could have taken action immediately, and rescued her from her predicament."

Rollison kept a straight face.

"Yes, indeed," he admitted. "But obviously I didn't make myself clear earlier in the evening, Inspector. I didn't want to bring the police into this business any more than I had to. I think that would make the situation worse. How long are you going to hold Miss Evans?"

"I cannot say until I have heard her answers to my questions."

"In that case I'd better lay on a lawyer," Rollison said briskly. "May I use a telephone at the station?"

"As Miss Evans has not yet been charged—"

"She's very young and inexperienced," Rollison pointed out, "and in her present state she might be misled into making a statement which could be misconstrued. Of course, if I can be present—"

"I doubt whether the interrogation will last more than ten minutes," said Nicholson, climbing down laboriously.

"If at any time Miss Evans feels that she needs advice I will permit her to nominate her own adviser."

"And you couldn't say fairer than that," said Rollison.

"We try to be fair to everyone, sir. According to reports, some members of the gang escaped at the back of the site, but no way out has been discovered. Are you aware of its location, Mr Rollison?"

"No," answered Rollison. "Find someone who knew the place when it was a Civil Defence Post. He'll know."

*　　*　　*

Doris was with Nicholson and two detective sergeants for a little under a quarter of an hour, and when she rejoined Rollison, who had waited in the charge-room, she was smiling her quiet, rather cynical smile, as if she was fully satisfied with the results of the interview. The station sergeant, who had been keeping a benevolent eye on Rollison, had also arranged for the hired Jaguar to be brought round to the station, and Nicholson, obviously for reasons of his own, did not repeat his questioning of Rollison. Rollison helped Doris into the car, went round and took the wheel, and drove off leisurely. He was undoubtedly watched by the many police on duty, and was sure that Ginger King and Pyne knew exactly where he was driving; and would know the moment he had left the East End. Once past Aldgate Pump, he felt able to relax more easily, and for the first time he glanced down at Doris, who had been sitting very still.

"Thank you, Doris," he said. "But why did you lie?"

"Surely you know," she said.

"I'd like to know more about what goes on in that mind of yours," Rollison told her, and as he glanced down he saw her lips curl, but she didn't look at him, only at the straight, narrow road which led to the Bank, the City and, far off, the West End where life began again. Here, London seemed both deserted and dead.

"Surely it's obvious," said Doris. "At your flat, Nicholson was as difficult as he could be, and I thought that if he could find an excuse he would probably charge you with inciting a riot or whatever he calls it. It seemed obvious that if I took the blame, he couldn't do anything to you."

"And you didn't want him to?"

"Naturally not."

"Why did you follow me?" asked Rollison.

"I didn't exactly follow you," she answered. "I thought you would go to see the Slob Mob, and I knew where their headquarters were, so I went and waited until you arrived. But I was scared—I did tell some of the truth!" This time there was an echo of nervous laughter in her voice. "Several of the Mob had seen me, and they watched me— I could have called out to you when you were parking your car, but I was too scared. Then just as you went into the club, they jumped me."

"So I gathered. How much more truth did you tell?" inquired Rollison.

"Well, I did rather like the look of Ginger this evening," Doris admitted, and now she turned to stare at Rollison; he was slowing down for the traffic lights at the Mansion House, and so could glance at her. She seemed very earnest, and the glow of the street lamps on her face softened a beauty which brighter light would have made hard. "And I did even when he was at the club, and when he was dancing. I was terrified when the others were pulling my clothes off, but I wasn't when I was dancing with Ginger."

"Did you know that he'd served three years in prison for robbery with violence?"

"Oh," ejaculated Doris, just as the lights changed. Rollison started off slowly, as Doris went on: "No, I didn't know. I'm surprised. I wouldn't put anything past that man who was with him, but Ginger—I can see him in a fight, but not—oh, well, it doesn't matter. I liked what I saw of him."

"Feel full of reforming zeal?" inquired Rollison.

"That is *not* clever."

"Probably not," said Rollison, "but this is as good a

time as any to tell you that the Ginger Kings of this part
of the world are the people I think it worth while working
on. Dorry, why did you come?"

"I've told you."

"Not everything."

"All that matters."

"I don't believe it," Rollison said, and went on firmly:
"Why was it? For the thrill? Did you feel a heroine,
venturing into the uncharted depths of the evil East End
all by yourself? Did you come simply to see what an East
End mob looks like when it's having fun? Or did you—"

"I've told you, I wanted to see Ginger again." Doris
hesitated, and then went on with a note of exasperation:
"I suppose the truth is I wanted to see what you would do
and how you would handle the situation. Jonas said that
he'd read that you'd once faced a crowd of two hundred
gangsters on your own, and I—well, I simply didn't believe there was anyone who had that kind of courage. I
had to find out."

Rollison chuckled.

"Very flattering," he said, "and yes, I believe you!
Doris, was it you who first suggested that the delegation
should come to see me?"

After a pause, she answered: "Yes."

"Why?"

"I had to do something."

"Life was too dull?"

"Toff," said Doris, and she shifted in her seat suddenly
so that she could see him more clearly, and she rested a
hand on his left arm, lightly; there was a tone of deeper
earnestness in her voice, and Rollison felt sure that she
was trying very hard to make him believe her. "Toff, I
told you everything, or Alec and Anne did for me. I *am*
tired of being treated like an imbecile. I *am* tired of being
told by school and college principals and teachers that I'm
still just a little girl. I *am* tired of the unbearably patronising air of nearly everyone who has anything to do with us,
and I *am* sick to death of student clubs, ping pong, dances

where you can't really rock in case the youth leader doesn't like to see your panties. Oh, they mean well, I suppose it's all right for a lot of kids, but I don't want that kind of organised existence, and very few of us do. We want to be something, do something, be given some credit. I expect it sounds corny to you but we're mostly seventeen, eighteen, or nineteen, old enough to fight wars, old enough to have babies, old enough to run homes, and—well, I thought you might be the one person who would see us as people and not as kids. *Are* you?"

Rollison's voice rose: "A kid? *You?*" He laughed as he turned into Trafalgar Square, where the fountains had ceased playing and the pigeons had gone to roost, but where a few people stood about, and throngs filled the window seats of the late night café nearby. "Dorry, my pet, you are a fully matured, desirable young woman, and you are absolutely right—the Slob Mob boys really react in much the same way as you do, but they have to work off their sense of injustice by organising into a crime band. Like what you've seen of it?"

Doris hesitated.

Rollison said: "I can drive you home, or we can go to my flat, where there's a comfortable spare room."

"I think I ought to go home," said Doris slowly, and then she laughed. Somehow she seemed much younger than when she had been talking so earnestly. "I'd much rather come and use your spare room! But Anne will be worried stiff, and I'm sure she wouldn't be satisfied with a telephone call. And they did get a crowd together and come after me; I owe them something."

"You owe them a lot, Dorry."

"Yes, I suppose so," Doris said. "Toff, the answer is that I don't know."

"Don't know what?"

"Whether I like what I've seen of the Slob Mob in action."

"Don't ever tell a policeman, a magistrate, or a social worker that," urged Rollison.

"I wouldn't dream of it," said Doris, "and yet—some-one ought to be told. I wouldn't tell Anne or the others, either, but the truth is that I'm not sure. There are some aspects of it that fascinate me. Believe it or not, I've never known youngsters dance like they did tonight. They put their whole heart, soul, and body into every jiggle, didn't they?"

"Yes."

"That's the thing that appeals to me about Ginger, and the reason why I'm not sure," said Doris, and Rollison was surprised as well as glad that she was being so absolutely frank. "They've got such vitality, and they enjoy what they're doing so much. Part of me hated being terrified, and yet there was a kind of fascination in it, too. Why, I— I felt almost hypnotised by Ginger! I've never known anyone hold me as tight as he did, he treated me as if I were something he'd bought and owned, and yet—I didn't really hate it."

Rollison made no comment, but turned into Birdcage Walk, watching the dark mass of Buckingham Palace and seeing the sentries on their inexorable march.

"Do you think I should have?" asked Doris.

13

HEADLINES

ROLLISON slowed down as he neared the open gates leading from Birdcage Walk, then pulled into the side of the road, switched off the engine, hitched himself round in his seat, and smiled at the girl. She was looking at him intently, almost imploringly, and he knew that she was desperately anxious for a soothing answer. He did not really know what to say. He could imagine Jolly, almost beside himself with impatience, saying that this girl's problem wasn't his, and up to a point that was right. If Rollison asked questions—how old she was, where her parents were, that kind of thing, she would take it for granted that he was being patronising; he needed the answers to the questions but had to find them out for himself, without her knowing. She was holding his hand very tightly, and that betrayed the tautness of her nerves. He remembered how calmly and coolly she had lied to Nicholson, and the possibility that she was fooling him came back to his mind. He did not reject it; he simply did not dwell on it.

"Let me put it this way," he said. "If the boot had been on the other foot, if I'd been grabbed by a really handsome, sexy, voluptuous female and made to think that she and I were the only two people in the world, I wouldn't have hated it. Twenty-five years ago I might have been a bit scared, but I would have echoed Jonas, brayed 'good-o!' and put her to the test."

"Put her to—oh, I see what you mean. Taken her to bed!"

Rollison chuckled.

"Or let her take me. And why assume that that's the only way of finding out whether a girl's for a man or a man's for a girl?" He paused for a moment, and then went on: "Scared by your own reaction, Doris?"

"I suppose I am, a bit."

"That's a healthy sign, surely. The man who worries me is the man who never gets frightened of himself. We all ought to, at some time or other. Now, let's see how things are. There's bound to be some kind of trouble after this, of course. If I know the Slob Mob, they will hit out pretty soon and somewhere unexpected, because they're on the crest of a wave. I don't quite know the internal set-up yet, but I think that a man named Pyne is pushing Ginger for all he's worth, and that Pyne is what we call a bad influence. I hope to find out more, very soon. What I don't want is another gang battle. If Jonas runs wild again— and I've never seen anyone fight with more guts—he could make trouble for a lot of your student friends, and I can imagine it going to their heads. Then they'd want nothing less than a pitched battle, which would be lunacy. It might be exciting while it lasted, but dozens would land in a police cell for a night to cool off, they might be remanded on bail, and when they came for trial the magistrate, if it went that far, might decide that they need teaching a lesson. Jonas and friends could find themselves in prison or in Borstal. Then everything that your principals and social advisers have prophesied would be proved true, which wouldn't help your generation or the two or three following you. Follow me?"

"Yes," said Doris slowly, and after a pause she went on: "But you don't know Jonas."

"Self-willed, is he?"

"Once he's started a thing he just won't let up," Doris declared. "He's one of the nicest people you could imagine, but—well, he simply won't sit back and do nothing. I'm sure he won't. And I certainly won't be able to persuade him to wait. Alec's the only one with any influence over him, but Alec's not likely to be about for a few days—you're quite right, he did have concussion."

"Pity," said Rollison. "All right—you stay close to our Jonas, and let me know what he's planning and what he wants to do. Let me know if he's got any crazy notion about a raid on the Slob Mob, for instance. Will you?"

She hesitated.

"Dorry," Rollison said, "believe it or not, you started all this."

"Yes, I know," Doris replied, and drew a deep breath. "Yes, all right, although I can't pretend that I enjoy acting as a spy. But I'll keep you in touch, and I'll try to calm Jonas down. He might be more ready to listen to you," she went on, thoughtfully. "He formed a high opinion of you."

"We'll use me as a last resort," said Rollison drily. He faced the road again, switched on the engine, and eased off the brake. "You won't tell any of your friends exactly what happened tonight, will you?"

"The strip-tease act? I'd never live it down!"

"Let's keep it between you, me, and the Slob Mob," said Rollison. "One other thing."

"Yes."

"How was it possible to organise the protest march this evening?"

"How—oh, I see what you mean, how did we get in touch with everyone? Well, there are several student associations, and technically we all belong to one. Anne and I roneo'd some messages and had them distributed at some of the colleges. It wasn't very different from organising a rag procession. We have to do a lot of that secretly, you know, making the floats and banners in odd corners where no one is likely to see the finished result until we're on the road, so we're quite used to getting banners ready. We used the Art College students for the lettering and the Woodwork School part-timers for the poles—it wasn't really a problem. Why?"

"I was thinking of the old saw about the Devil and idle hands," said Rollison. "You people want something to do but you don't yet know exactly what it is. If we could find out—but I'd better be careful, or I'll be preaching. Exactly where is this flat of yours?"

The flat was in an old house in a road of terraced houses near the boundary of Fulham and Chelsea. Lights were on at three of the front windows, and several old cars were parked in the streets; probably cars owned by the students. Rollison helped Doris out of his car, and as she stood up, someone called from a doorway:

"There she is!"

"Dorry!" a youngster called. "Are we glad to see you!" A little group of students came hurrying forward. "Jonas is upstairs threatening to raid all London to find you, and—oh! Mr Rollison."

"Doris has been making sure I didn't get caught and sent to prison," said Rollison lightly. "Good night, Doris. Good night, all."

He got into the car and drove off on a chorus of good nights, after watching the little crowd surround Doris and escort her into the house where she lived. He pictured Jonas Lee, getting mad and violent enough to want to lead another raid on the East End in order to find her. Whether he, Rollison, could have prevented this had he received the delegation differently was unimportant: what mattered was dealing with the situation and making sure that it didn't deteriorate. Given Jonas and a few more hotheads in the Fulham, Chelsea, Kensington, and Victoria areas, then the situation could become very ugly indeed.

Rollison drove to Gresham Terrace, where there was ample room to park at night, and thought fleetingly that if he had driven to the East End in his own car, which was garaged nearby, he might have got to the Slob Mob's headquarters in time to see Doris when she had arrived. He still wondered what really went on in her mind, to make her venture as she had that night, and he could recall the almost wistful tone of her voice when she had told him that she had not hated the 'dance' with Ginger; and when she had asked whether he thought that she should have. He smiled to himself as he opened the street door, hesitated, made sure that no one was inside the hall, and that the lights were on at all the landings. He reached his own landing as Jolly opened the door, still fully dressed, looking only a little tired.

"Hello, Jolly," Rollison said. "What's the nearest thing you can find me to a Turkish bath?"

"Now, sir?" Jolly was very slightly surprised.

"Now, or I'll be as stiff as a horse in the morning," said Rollison, "and I don't think that would be so good. I have some news for you. I danced with a teenager with the wildest abandon tonight, and she collapsed first." He stretched and felt the twinges of pain at his legs and his arms, and then yawned. "I wish it weren't necessary," he said, "but I'm sure it is."

"I think the best thing is for you to have a hot bath with plenty of Epsom salts in it; I have a seven pound bag for the purpose," Jolly said. "Then I will give you a rub down afterwards."

"It's late, Jolly."

"Only a little after midnight," said Jolly. "I will run the bath. No—er—serious injury, sir?"

"None."

"Mr Ebbutt telephoned me about an hour ago and told me that you were at the divisional police station," said Jolly, "and he also gave me some indication of what had happened. I was a little troubled in case the police should detain you."

"Troubled? Or hopeful?"

Jolly turned in the doorway leading to the domestic quarters, hesitated, and then gave a smile which delighted Rollison, for there was so much warmth in it, and so much affection—and great understanding, too. It was in such moments as these that he realised how much he owed to Jolly and just what his man meant to him. Thirty years of close association could break down all barriers; it was Jolly who kept some of the barriers up.

"No, sir," Jolly said, "I had no desire to have you cooling your heels in jug! As a matter of fact I have been thinking about our conversation very deeply, and I have been trying to see the point of view of these young people. Also, I skimmed through some of the newspapers in our files, and read some of the comments about youth from their mentors. A number of them really are ludicrous, I will admit. I can't honestly say that I accept your point of view, but I do understand it—I assure you that I do. And I can also agree with you this far: if it is possible to avoid open trouble with this Slob Mob, it would be a good thing. Would you like anything before your bath, sir?"

"No, thanks," said Rollison, humbly. "A ham sandwich when you've tucked me up in bed, that's all."

He was glad to take off the vest, but very grim-faced when he saw the brightness where the knife had scraped the linked metal. In a mirror, with Jolly to hold it in position, he saw the bruise caused by the knife.

"Just thanks, Jolly," he said.

He soaked for a quarter of an hour, Jolly pummelled and gave him electric massage for twenty minutes, and he felt physically tired and mentally alert when he got into bed, and had the ham sandwich and drank tea; it had been a recent trick of coffee to keep him awake at night. He settled down at half past one, feeling almost sure that he would not get to sleep for some time—and woke, a little after nine o'clock, to find Jolly entering the room with the morning tea tray, and with a sheaf of newspapers under his arm.

"Hello, Jolly," Rollison said, and stifled a yawn as he began to recall what had happened, and the mists of sleep receded. "What kind of"—he yawned again—"Press have we got?"

"An extensive one," replied Jolly, and put the tray down by the Toff's side. "I think it true to say that we have more space than the Wimbledon murders, the Japanese earthquake, the threatened rail strike, and the Royal family at the theatre. You—ah—appear in most of the headlines."

"Pity," said Rollison, and sat up and took the newspapers while Jolly poured out tea.

There he was: at the shattered window, at the street door, talking to the police. There were the headlines—YOUTH ATTACKS TOFF—TOFF IN HOT WATER—GANG WAR IN MAYFAIR. There was a fair variety of headlines, and most of the pictures were good; each newspaper had chosen one which showed him with the streak of blood across his forehead. Very little was said about the actual protest march, although there were some pictures of the marchers and the banners. The best pictures were of the Slob Mob members flinging their missiles at Rollison's flat, and some of these were brilliant. Rollison studied them closely, looking for likenesses of Ginger King and Pyne; and when he found them he studied each with close attention. Nothing changed his opinion about Pyne, but he found himself looking, in Ginger King, for the quality of attractiveness which Doris seemed to find in him.

Jolly said: "I wouldn't have called you so early, sir, but there will be half-a-dozen newspapermen here at ten o'clock and Detective Inspector Nicholson is due at half past ten. I felt it wise for you to be in to all of them."

"Quite right," Rollison said. "Thanks, Jolly. And I don't think I'm going to be too stiff, either, the Epsom's worked wonders. Any news from anywhere?"

"You mean from Miss Evans or the others?"

"Yes."

"No news, sir, except that the young man Price is likely to be in hospital for some time. There is a suspected fracture of the skull, and he is nothing like so well as we would hope."

Rollison said, heavily: "That all?"

"I don't quite understand, sir."

"Are you telling me that Price is on the danger list?"

"I wasn't told so in those words, sir, but I did understand that he is more seriously injured than was at first suspected—apparently he had considerable hemorrhage during the night. Mr Harrison obtained the information and told me, and I called the hospital just before coming in to you."

"Oh," said Rollison, still heavily. "The others all right?"

"As far as I know, sir," answered Jolly.

14

COUNCIL OF WAR

RAY HARRISON's curly hair and fresh complexion made him look even more boyish when he arrived at the flat, just before ten o'clock, but he had nothing more to tell the Toff than Jolly had already reported. With the five other reporters on his heels, he made one thing clear: this was a news item of the first degree. The editors of all the national and of many provincial newspapers were whipping up the interest. Editorials were coming out by the dozen. The theme of all of them was the same: the nation was approaching a time when the Youth of Great Britain was Planning to Defy Society. In other parts of the world there had been serious eruptions of teenage violence, but so far most of the eruptions in this country had been confined to certain poorer parts of London and the big cities. Now it appeared as if that was spreading to residential areas.

What did the Toff think?

Why had he talked so freely earlier in the week? Had he been uttering a warning?

Had he in fact been working on this problem for longer than anyone yet realised? Had he gone to see the Chelham students or had they come to see him? Was there any truth in the story that a Chelham girl had been snatched by the Slob Mob, and made to do a strip-tease? The questions were shot at Rollison from all directions, and he answered those he wanted to, and stalled where that seemed wise. One thing was apparent: they had all failed to get an interview with Doris Evans, although Jonas Lee had proved unexpectedly garrulous with one newspaperman.

The Press were still at the flat when Nicholson arrived from the Yard. Obviously he had been warned of this by men stationed in the street, and he showed unexpected blandness and skill in answering questions about the battle in Whale Street the previous night. His favourite phrase was: "Not to my knowledge." It was nearly eleven o'clock before the newspapermen went off. Then Nicholson, on his own—which meant that he still did not intend to make this too formal—turned that unwinking gaze upon the Toff, and asked:

"Are you aware that Alec Price's injury is very serious?"

"Yes," Rollison said.

"Have you seen Doris Evans this morning?"

"No."

"Or Jonas Lee? Or the other girl, Anne Darby?"

"No."

"Have you arranged to see them?"

"Not specifically," Rollison said. "Why these questions, Inspector? What difference would it make either way?"

"I am desirous of knowing whether the Chelham students are plotting a return visit to Whale Street," said Nicholson. "My information is that instructions have been given to the Slob Mob to lie low for several days. In fact I think it possible that they will be inactive for several weeks. The authorities have an informant among their ranks," he added, and for the first time it seemed to Rollison that there was a hint of a twinkle in the pale grey eyes. "I was informed on good authority exactly what happened at the club last night."

"Ah."

"Did Ginger King assault the Evans girl?"

"No," said Rollison, quietly. "No—others roughed her up a bit, but not Ginger."

"I see. Do you regard it as probable that the Chelham students will attempt some form of reprisal for what happened to Miss Evans?"

"They might."

"My understanding is that the Australian, Jonas Lee, is the firebrand among them, although there are occasions when he appears to be virtually dumbstruck," said

Nicholson. "I am informed that he will go into a fight utterly regardless of the risks or consequences, and is quite fearless. However, he is not accustomed to the weapons which the Slob Mob might use, nor to their ruthlessness. To him a fight is still a sporting occasion, rather like a conflict between two groups of schoolboys, and I have reason to believe that he has no real conception of the dangers which this situation could give rise to."

"Ah," said Rollison.

"Mr Rollison, do you expect Lee to lead the Chelham students into the East End?"

"I'm doing my damnedest to make sure that he doesn't."

"I am very glad to hear it," Nicholson said, fervently. "I have been discussing this matter with my superiors, including Chief Superintendent Grice."

"Good," approved Rollison.

"Mr Grice has told me that he is sure that you will act with the best possible motives and that your knowledge of the East End is great enough to demand great respect," said Nicholson. "But at the same time he suggests that you might possibly be out of touch."

Rollison exclaimed: "*What?*"

"You haven't spent much time in the East End of late, sir, have you—except among your friends?"

Rollison replied slowly: "No. No, not a great deal."

"It is Mr Grice's considered opinion that you may have under-estimated the viciousness and the cunning of some members of the Slob Mob, and he would be very sorry indeed to find that you had been injured. It was my duty to inform him that it has come to my notice that certain threats were made last night against your person—to wit, threats to murder you."

Rollison said: "Oh, has it?"

"Is that true, sir?"

"If I had a pound for every threat against my life I'd be a wealthy man."

"I have reason to believe that the man who uttered this

threat is clever and dangerous, sir. According to my information, which cannot yet be substantiated, the man is Harry Pyne. According to the information lodged by doctors who examined Pyne on two occasions in the past, once when he was eleven and was charged with causing bodily harm to a four-year-old child, and once when he was fifteen when he was accused of inciting to violence, this man Pyne is an extremely dangerous psychopath."

Rollison said: "Nicholson, you certainly get around."

"It's my job to, sir," said Nicholson, with devastating simplicity. "And I don't want to see you hurt any more than Mr Grice does."

"Thank you."

"Further, sir, my information is that after your remarkable—er—can I say performance?—last night, Pyne regards you as a threat to his ascendancy over the Slob Mob. I understand that he believed that you created far too favourable an impression on many of the members of the Mob, and that he wishes to eradicate that impression."

Rollison said thoughtfully: "Yes, it fits, but—where do you get information like this, Nicholson?"

"I have my sources, sir."

"Do you know how the Slob Mob first heard of the procession?"

"A local newspaperman passed the word on, sir."

"I see. You couldn't be trying to scare me off because I won't be warned, could you?"

Nicholson looked bovinely astonished. "I assure you, sir, I am telling you the simple truth. My contact is in fact a girl close to one of the leading members of the Mob. She takes great risks to keep me informed, and—"

"Nicholson."

"Mr Rollison?"

"Who is she?"

"I cannot disclose her name."

"Between these walls, remember."

Nicholson hesitated, and then said slowly: "I cannot

see that it will do any harm, Mr Rollison, but I give you this information in the strictest confidence. The person is a girl named Jacobs, a friend of Ginger King. Does that satisfy you, sir?"

"Yes," said Rollison. "I suppose it has to. Thanks. What are you asking me to do?"

"Do nothing to encourage the Chelham students to raid the East End," said Nicholson. "And inform me if at any time there appears to be the slightest risk that Jonas Lee will lead a party into the area." He paused, raised his hands in front of him as if to indicate that he hadn't yet finished, then he gave a broad, slow, attractive smile, and went on: "In addition, sir, I would be very grateful if you would give some thought to the possible ways of creating a permanent cure for the Slob Mob disease. If these people could be given some sense of purpose in which they could use up their surplus energy and their ingenuity—something which would not appear to them as being conventional and ordinary, if you see what I mean."

"I do indeed," said Rollison. "Do you know what I think about that?"

"No, sir."

"We could try to use the Chelham youngsters, who might understand the Slob Mob better than we do. Let's see what we've got to go on. Harry Pyne is the real danger. You think he might mean to kill me, because he's worried about the reaction of this crowd, and he'll certainly want to discredit me."

"That's quite right, sir."

"And you want to try and make sure that there's a real armistice for a couple of weeks, anyhow."

"I think that sums it up exactly," said Nicholson. "Thank you very much."

Rollison saw him off, went back to his room, contemplated the Trophy Wall for several minutes, especially the hangman's rope and the curate's collar. That old gang war seemed to be very vivid in his mind, and he wondered what the curate, now in South Africa on another sticky wicket, would do in the present circumstances. He wondered, also, if he could rely on Doris warning him of any plan to raid the East End. He was still a long way from certain about what went on in Doris Evans's mind, and by this morning she might have recovered from last night's scare.

Then he pulled up his chair, lifted his telephone, dialled Ebbutt, and asked Ebbutt to find out all he could about Harry Pyne.

"I don't mind telling you I've been diggin' a bit already," said Ebbutt, "and I don't like wot I 'ear, Mr Ar. Very nasty bit o' work, that Pyne, very nasty. And I was going to call you anyway, Mr Ar."

"Why, Bill?"

"Well, there's a rumour going around that Pyne's going to do you proper," Ebbutt told him. "You know how these things go, doncher? Seems like you give him a nasty kick in the pants lars night—he didn't like the way the Mob took to you. I've heard all abaht it," Ebbutt went on, with satisfaction and no little pride, "and you can take it from me, you've got to look aht. 'Arry Pyne's dangerous."

"Where can I find him by day, Bill?" inquired Rollison.

"Now, Mr Ar—"

"Don't hold out on me," ordered Rollison.

Ebbutt sounded very wheezy as he hesitated, and even wheezier when at last he answered:

"He's got a room above Girodo's caff, in the Mile End Road, Mr Ar. It's a pop'lar place, always plenty of young swabs about there—it's an unofficial meeting place for the Slob Mob. Mr Ar, you want to be careful, very careful."

"Bill, I will be," promised Rollison. "Think you could get a list of the names and addresses of the Slob Mob for me?"

Ebbutt hesitated, still wheezily. Then:

"Well, most of 'em, Mr Ar. I don't suppose there's no

such list in existence, but me and my boys could make one up from mem'ry. When do you want it?"

"I'd like an envelope addressed to each Slob, by ten o'clock tonight."

"Tell you wot, Mr Ar," said Ebbutt, "I'll do the best I can. Want me to bring 'em to you?"

"I'll come to the gym just after ten," promised Rollison. "But don't be surprised if you don't recognise me."

"I'd reckernise you dressed as a Russian ballet dancer," Ebbutt declared. "Okay, I'll fix it."

"Thanks, Bill," said Rollison, and rang off before Ebbutt could repeat any warning. He hesitated for a few moments, reflectively, then pressed the bell push at his desk, the one which would summon Jolly. Jolly came in at once, but gave the impression that he was preoccupied, probably with the making of pastry; there was a smear of flour on his right cheek. "Jolly," Rollison said, "I want your services as a make-up artist. Forget lunch, and let's get busy."

"In your usual guise, sir?" inquired Jolly.

"In the guise of a dock labourer who hates the world and the police in particular," Rollison said. "Although it might be better if I were just off a ship. That's it, I'll be a merchant seaman. We'd better find out what ships have come in this morning. Can you make me look like a merchant seaman, Jolly?"

"I must admit that the more I see of this affair the less I like it, sir," said Jolly, "but yes, of course I can. The necessary clothes are in the maplewood wardrobe. I think it would be wise to make sure that the boots fit, sir, or to wear an old pair of your ordinary make. I hope you will travel armed."

"It's a long time since I have," said Rollison, "but yes— I will. Armed and armoured. And afterwards, I shall want about a hundred visiting cards, the old model, all stamped with the top hat sign, and ready for slipping into envelopes . . ."

*   *   *

It was in the middle of that afternoon when Harry Pyne opened the door of his room above Girodo's Café, to admit Ginger King and the man named Smith, who had been discharged from Vine Street that morning because no charge had been preferred against him. Girodo had been discharged, too. Smith's close-shaven head made him look almost grotesque as he followed Ginger. Girodo, son of the proprietor of the café, was not in the inner council of the Slob Mob; he was now acting as look-out man, to warn the others if suspicious strangers entered the café, or if the place were being kept under surveillance—by rival gangs or by the police.

The room was quite large, and was unexpectedly well-furnished. Leading off it was a bathroom, and a tiny kitchenette, although Harry Pyne had most of his food sent up from the café.

The furniture in the room itself was contemporary, with a somewhat Scandinavian simplicity; the colours were red, black, and grey, and the carpet was a zig-zag design in all three. In one corner was a loud, stereophonic radiogram, with racks of records above it, reaching almost to the low ceiling. The dining-table had a slender, fragile look, surrounded by four chairs with spiky iron legs. The three men took a chair apiece, and Pyne pushed cigarettes and matches across the shiny table. In some ways this was like a board meeting, and many limited companies had less attractive meeting places.

"Well, Harry boy," Ginger said, "what's the business today?" When Pyne did not reply at once, he went on a little uneasily: "That right you passed the word round to lay off for a bit?"

Pyne said: "Yes, it is."

"But Harry—"

"We lay off because we want to make the Toff's mob start something first," said Pyne. "That's what we want, Ginger boy. I know what we want all right." He looked at Smith as if defying him to deny the wisdom of that, and when only silence met him, he went on: "The way to do it is to prod them hard, see. Make 'em mad as hell. Make 'em start it. Then Rollison will come to try to get them out of their trouble. Then we'll get Rollison, and—"

"Listen, Harry—" Ginger began.

"Let me say my piece, Ginger boy," interrupted Pyne with a great show of heartiness. "You haven't gone far wrong in taking my advice so far, have you?"

"S'true enough," Ginger admitted.

"Done okay, Ginger," said Smith.

"So keep taking my advice until I've let you down," said Pyne, and added with a thin-lipped smile: "That means you'll be taking it for a hell of a long time, Ginger boy." He spread his hands out on the table, palms downward, and looked at Ginger with his dark eyes. They seemed to become larger, seemed to glow, and Ginger felt a strange effect from them, as he often did. Pyne's voice took on a low-pitched, almost a sing-song tone as he went on: "Now listen, Ginger. We want to make the Slob Mob the most powerful ever. That right?" The others nodded. "We want you to go on record as the biggest leader ever. Right?" Ginger moistened his lips and nodded again. "So how are you going to do it? Why do you think I advised the Mob to go up West last night? Because of one man, see—this Rollison. Rollison hasn't been around in the East End so much lately, but you can take it from me, he's a copper's nark—he's just a stool pigeon, that's all Rollison is. But he's the biggest name in the East End of London, bar none. You don't need telling that, Ginger, do you? The cops, the shopkeepers, the clubs—they're all for Rollison. He's got them where he wants them, that's the truth, he's got 'em in the palm of his hand.

"Let me tell you something." Pyne leaned forward, hands clenching now, and voice pitched so low that the others had to strain their ears to catch his words: "For over twenty bloody years that man's been around in this part of London, when he belongs to the other part. He's put more of our chaps inside than anyone else, except the cops—he's put ten inside for any one by any single copper, too. Why, there are some of our own Mob members who've been inside, or whose old men have been inside, simply because of Rollison. If you fix Rollison, Ginger, you'll be the real big shot in our part of London. Don't make any mistake about that—fix Rollison, get rid of him for everyone, and you'll be the accepted leader not only of the Mob but every gang in the big smoke. You'll really be the top man, Ginger. It's not often a chap gets a chance like you, but you've got this one, and Rollison's made it for you. See why I suggested going there now? See what I mean? See how you can be the biggest thing in the East End of London if you kill the Toff—or if you make him useless. That's what we've got to fix," went on Pyne, and now he clenched his hands so tightly that it looked as if it hurt him. "We've got to find a way of wiping the Toff off the face of the earth and making sure the cops can't get us for it. That's the job, Ginger, that's why we're here. Now, listen . . ."

15

VISITING CARDS

HALF past three in the afternoon was not the busiest time for Girodo's Café, although there were always a few people there from the nearby meat wholesale warehouses, mostly big men with bloodstained white aprons and loud voices, each capable of carrying a whole side of beef from the back of a refrigerated room to the front of a refrigerated van. A few drivers, one or two hawkers, and some barrow men were also there, but very few youngsters; most of the teenagers did some kind of work. It was not until the early evening that the café was virtually taken over by the gang.

Old Tino Girodo knew exactly what was going on, and his conscience did not trouble him; the Slob Mob brought him more money, more trade, and more profit than he had known before in his twenty years as a café owner, and he was all in favour. It might have been different had his wife not died, five years earlier. Since her death Tino Girodo had cared only about making money, and about his son Luigi; he wanted to see Luigi a big shot, and believed that the youth was on the way up.

Tino had double reason to be grateful to the Mob, because they gave him a form of protection as well as extra business. They did not want the police to raid their own social headquarters and committee room, so at Girodo's their behaviour was reasonably good. The police, knowing who spent so much time there, watched it constantly, but they were never given any cause to take action. Rival gangs, such as Taggarty's, would never stage a raid here, because it was so close to Aldgate Station and the main roads leading to the East coast; if anyone started trouble the police could be in action within a few minutes and in great strength. Girodo believed that the café was the safest place in all London, and felt sure that Ginger King and Pyne thought the same thing; otherwise, why meet here?

Strangers were not uncommon in the afternoon.

When a tall, heavy-looking stranger came in, wearing a narrow cap with a shiny peak, and a reefer jacket which had an American or a continental look about it, Tino took no particular notice. He waited until the man came up to the counter and contemplated the sandwiches, cheese-cakes, dough-nuts, and cheese rolls inside several spotlessly clean glass containers. Tino, short and plump, with very black hair plastered thinly over a shiny white pate, stood with the hot water urn bubbling and chuckling behind him. The only other people here were two men from Butchers' Row, and one elderly woman who was going to start cleaning work at a wholesaler's later in the afternoon.

"Whatta you want, mister?" Tino asked, civilly.

"Can I get a hot meal?" the sailor asked. He had a slightly American accent, and might well be a Canadian, Tino judged. "Bacon and eggs, maybe, and some French fries."

"Sure, sure," Tino said. "You waita for five minutes, I cooka bacon an' eggs. You sitta there, or you go to a table?"

"I'll sit here," said the stranger.

"Sure, mister," Tino said. "You wanta cuppa char to start?"

"What's that?"

"You wanta cup tea or coffee, mister?"

"I want bacon and eggs, Big Boy."

"Sure, mister, right away," said Tino, and he hurried to the room behind the café, where he had a gas stove and could do simple cooking, and yet hear if anyone came in.

By the stranger's right elbow was a large pile of folded paper serviettes, and he took a dozen or so small cards from his pocket and slipped a card in between the folds of a dozen or so serviettes from the top of the pile. He could not be seen; and even if anyone chanced to see what he was doing it would look as if he was helping himself to a serviette. It was more difficult to stretch out so that he could take some of the ham sandwiches from the glass container, without being noticed, but he did so skilfully, and placed a card inside each of six sandwiches—again starting towards the bottom of the pile. By the time he had finished and had replaced the sandwiches and the glass cover, Tino Girodo came bustling with a piping hot plate of bacon, eggs, and golden brown chips.

The stranger took his time eating, then had two cups of coffee and a doughnut, and left the café about four o'clock. No one took any notice of him, so no one saw him stroll across the road, cross at the first zebra crossing, and take a window seat at another café, almost opposite Girodo's.

*　　*　　*

Upstairs, the committee meeting finished a little after five o'clock, and Ginger, Pyne, and Smith came downstairs, strolling into the café as if they owned the whole establishment. By then, young Luigi was serving the few customers. The door opened and a group of four youths surged in, all of whom had been at Whale Street the night before, all with the kind of swagger which was calculated to drive older people out of the café. Two of them went to a pin ball machine, and the lights began to flash and the bells to ring. Two more went to a juke box, and sixpences began to disappear, remote-controlled robotclaws moved, and a record clattered down on the turntable. Cups, saucers, and plates clattered, doughnuts, cheese cakes with their topping of shredded coconut, even ham sandwiches began to disappear, and the piles of the paper serviettes went down quite quickly.

The stranger strolled across from the other café, and came back into this one. No one took any notice of him, except Harry Pyne; Pyne missed nothing and no one. He saw an unshaven rough-looking individual, with bulgy looking nostrils and very lean cheeks wearing the shiny peaked cap and the un-English lumber jacket. The man ordered coffee, and took it to a corner table.

Old Tino was off duty and would be for a couple of hours, a chance which the Toff, who looked so much like a sailor just off his ship, had not reckoned on; he usually had some luck.

Pyne looked away from him, apparently unsuspicious, strolled across to the juke box as the last of three records stopped, put in two shillings for four records, selected pop tunes, and strolled back to the glass-topped table. By now, twenty or more of the Slob Mob were present, the café was steamy and hot. Several girls had joined them and were sitting together. Snide remarks began to pass to and fro, the air was filled with smoke. "Hi, Charley; Hi, Harry?" "How're you, Ginger Boy?" mingled with: "Kate looks as if she was aht on the tiles last night, don't she?" The men made few references to the fight and the police raid. There was a kind of unwritten law: that they would discuss 'business' only among themselves unless it was to gloat over a victory.

It was one of the girls, a brunette with greasy-looking hair which spilled down over her shoulders, who first mentioned Rollison.

"Daisy, how about that Toff, last night? Bit of all right, weren't 'e?"

"You're telling me!"

"Proper Gregory Peck, that's what he was," another girl said. "Now if he was to ask me—"

She stopped. In a strange, hypnotic way, Harry Pyne contrived to make her. She looked away from him quickly, and a moment of disquiet seemed to touch everyone in the room. Then the music started up again and the voices were raised louder, the girl began to giggle at a lewd story which a few years earlier could never have been heard outside a smoking room for men only. Then across the cackle, the cacophony, and the high spirits there came a single expletive:

"*Jeese!*"

It was a fair-haired boy with a face rather like an angel's. He was sitting at a table in the middle of the room, a cup of coffee and a ham sandwich in front of him. The top of the sandwich had been removed—because he had been unable to cut through it with a knife. A card lay there, and the side towards him showed a little picture, obviously a rubber stamp impression, of a top hat on a man without a face. A monocle covered one eye, a dot served for the other, a cigarette holder jutted at a jaunty angle from the place where the mouth should be, and a bow tie completed the illusion of a face which was not there.

"The blinking *Toff*!" the fair-haired youth gasped.

"The—*Toff*?" someone echoed, and looked round uneasily.

Harry Pyne stood up from his chair, very deliberately, and stalked across the room. Ginger, less resolute, stood up but did not follow. Dank-haired, thin-faced, open-mouthed, Luigi Girodo watched, from behind the counter. Pyne reached the fair-haired youth's table and stared down at the card.

After a moment, he looked at Girodo, and said: "How many more of these have you got?"

"*I—I—I* haven't—" began Girodo, suddenly nervous.

"Who put it there?" demanded Pyne, and for a moment it looked as if he did not know how to keep his temper. "You lousy slob, *who put it there?*"

"Harry, I dunno nothin' about it! I tell you I dunno—"

Pyne swung round the end of the counter, lifted the lid of a container, snatched up three more sandwiches, and flipped the top layer of bread off. On three sandwiches the man without a face stared blankly up at him. All the colour drained from his cheeks, and his eyes became more luminous and yet more dark. His jaw bones began to work, and he clenched his hands until the skin was white at his knuckles.

"How many more?" he demanded, and when Girodo simply stood gaping at him, he opened his hand and slapped the youth across the face. *"Answer me?* How many more of these did you put in here?"

"Harry, I swear to you—"

One of the girls screamed: *"Eeeeehh!"* in a high-pitched screech, which made everyone swing round, even Harry Pyne. Everyone in the café was staring at the girl, gaping down at her lap. Pyne raised both hands, but stood absolutely still.

"What is it?" he demanded. "What's going on?"

The girl said: "It—it just fell out of my serviette. I—I opened it, and it fell out."

"What fell out?"

The girl put her hands to her skirt, and picked up another of the cards showing that man without a face. She held it up so that Pyne could see. He stared at it, his lips compressed into one thin line. Ginger moved towards him, heavily. Girodo picked up three more paper serviettes and shook them; cards fluttered to the floor, there was a faint fluttering sound. Pyne watched them go, and then turned to Ginger King and said in a thin, penetrating voice:

"See what I mean?"

"I can see," Ginger said. "But how did they get there, that's what I want to know. Who put them there?"

"If it wasn't Luigi, it was his old man," Harry Pyne said. "Go get your Pa," he ordered Luigi Girodo.

"Listen, Harry—"

"Go get your old man."

"Snap out of it, Harry," Ginger said, in a sharper voice than normal. "Maybe the Toff put these cards here himself, he's a clever geezer, you said so yourself. Luigi and Tino wouldn't do a thing like this."

"Let's have the old man here, to find out," said Pyne, viciously. "Let's see how much he was paid to—"

"Harry, listen to me! No one knows who put them there!" cried Girodo. "I swear it. My pa wouldn't do a thing like that, you know he wouldn't."

"Okay, Luigi, forget it," Ginger said. "Okay, Harry,

forget it. So the Toff paid a visit and left his card. So what? We can leave our card on him again, can't we?" He grinned, unexpectedly. "He's a bright boy, that Rollison, he—"

Pyne said in a low-pitched voice: "He's the most dangerous man in London to us, that's what Rollison is. Any man who can put Rollison where he belongs will be all right with me." He turned away from the counter, tacitly giving way without withdrawing his accusation against the Girodos. The girl continued to stare at the card. The fair-haired boy held his, then began to slide it into his pocket. Pyne strode over, snatched the card from him, ripped it across and across and flung the little pieces into the air. "Come on, let's have the lot," he ordered, and glanced at Ginger almost as if he expected further argument. But Ginger's eyes lit up. He snatched a card from a youth who had picked one from the floor and tore it into tiny pieces, others took them from sandwiches, the pile of serviettes vanished and more cards fluttered from them as they were tossed in the air. There was a furious but harmless orgy of tearing the cards across and across—and during the height of it, the merchant sailor got up and went out. No one really noticed him, for the other older people had gone out already, as if to make sure that they were not caught up in any trouble.

The 'sailor' went into a telephone kiosk at Aldgate Station, and dialled a Mayfair number, and a man answered promptly:

"This is the residence of the Honorable Richard Rollison."

"Jolly," said the man who had spoken with such a good north American accent, "the first card trick was a complete success. I'll need some more ready tonight, and I'll need a change of jacket and cap, to avoid being recognised. Ask Ebbutt to have envelopes addressed to all the people on the list he's preparing for me, will you?"

"Very good, sir," said Jolly.

"Thanks. How are things with you?"

"The only thing to report is a message from Miss Evans," answered Jolly. "She asked me to tell you that she thinks that Jonas Lee will listen to reason for today, at least."

"He'd better," said Rollison, mildly. "I'll look in for dinner, Jolly." After a pause, he added: "But I'll have to be away at half past nine, to collect those envelopes from Ebbutt. It ought to be quite a busy night."

16

SECOND CARD TRICK

BILL EBBUTT sat in the small, wooden partitioned cubicle which he called an office, and studied some papers through the tiny rims of his *pince nez*. He was a massive man with an enormous torso, and he had once been a very good heavyweight boxer. Now he trained and reared champions in this gymnasium, where a dozen hopes were climbing the parallel bars, vaulting the horses, thumping the punchball, skipping or sparring. Ebbutt himself did little more than keep a fatherly eye on his protegés, for two of the trainers in the gymnasium were excellent judges of a boxer. At that time no one of exceptional promise was under Ebbutt's wing, and he was studying a boxing newspaper, trying to find some ways of matching his boys without letting them get hurt too badly. In Ebbutt's opinion, nothing ruined a boy's chances of eventual success like an early beating-up. The noises of slapping, slipping, and thudding came clearly, there was a slight odour of wood from sawdust in the ring.

Everything here was new or newish, for not long ago the gymnasium had been wrecked by a mob of older men than the Slobs; soon afterwards every friend that Ebbutt and Rollison had in the East End had contributed towards its rebuilding. Even the office, once a litter of papers, pens, cigarette ash, and tickets, was passably tidy. Ebbutt sat on a square leather-topped stool, overlapping it at each edge, aware of what was going on outside even when a man came to the door and spoke to Percy Wrightson, one of the older members of this unofficial club. Wrightson's special distinction was that he occasionally acted as stand-in for Jolly at Rollison's Mayfair flat, for Wrightson was not a bad cook. He talked to the stranger for half a minute or so, then walked briskly to Ebbutt's office. He was a small, thin man who looked too weak to stand up, but in his frail-looking arms he packed a remarkable punch.

"What's it, Percy?" demanded Ebbutt.

"Cove 'ere wants ter see yer."

"Whattabaht?"

"Says he's got a boy you can do sunning with."

"Where's the boy?"

"Dunno."

"Better 'ave a word wiv 'im, you never know," said Ebbutt. "Send 'em over." He turned back to the boxing paper, then carefully tucked a list of names and addresses inside a drawer; this was the list which Rollison had asked him to prepare, and he believed that with the help of Percy and several others it was almost complete. The addressed envelopes, all typewritten, were in two packets in the drawer.

Wrightson led the tough-looking man over, and Ebbutt watched him over the top of the rimless glasses. This man had rather a broad nose, especially at the nostrils, his cheeks seemed sunken, and he hadn't shaved that day. He walked with a rolling kind of gait which suggested the seafarer.

"Here's the cove, Bill," Wrightson said.

"Okay, mister," Ebbutt said. "Wot's this about a good boy? I'm always in'trested in—"

"You're a bright pair, you are," the stranger said in a whispering voice but one which could be only the Toff's. "I always said you needed new glasses, Bill."

There was a moment's absolute silence. Then:

"*Blimey!*" exclaimed Ebbutt, explosively.

"Of all the flickin'—" began Wrightson.

"Not so much noise," said Rollison hastily. "I don't want the others to know who I am. Have any luck with that Slob Mob list, Bill?"

Dazedly, Ebbutt drew the list out of the drawer, and handed it over. Unbelievingly, Wrightson stared at the face which should have been so familiar but which Jolly had helped to alter so that it was that of a stranger. Neither men knew that suction pads pulled Rollison's cheeks in, that grease paint shaded the eyes cunningly and altered their shape and seemed to alter their colour, that plastic at the nostrils so changed the Toff's aristocratic nose.

He took the list.

"Wonderful, Bill. Thanks."

"What are you going to do with it, now you've got it?" demanded Ebbutt, recovering a little from the shock.

"Put a card in every letter box on the list," Rollison said. "Any luck with the envelopes too, Bill?"

"Yes, they're ready," said Ebbutt, and gulped, and then sneezed. "Sorry," he gasped, and his gaze was puzzled when he went on: "Mr Ar, why don't you let some of my boys do this job for you? They'd do it like a shot, and it would be just the same as if you'd done it yourself."

"They'd certainly do it better," said Rollison, "but this has to be from me to the Slob Mob."

"Who'd know the difference?" demanded Ebbutt.

"Everyone who sees me putting one of these in a letter box will describe the same man," said Rollison, "and when it's done I'm going to have a little talk with Harry Pyne."

Ebbutt, sliding off his stool, said huskily: "Mr Ar, I dunno whether you ought to do this, I don't really. The more I hear about Pyne, the less I like it. I wouldn't try to fool you, Mr Ar, but that chap's bad."

"That's what the police say, Bill."

"Then this is one time when they're right. Mr Ar—"

"Bill," said Rollison very firmly, "you can't talk me out of it."

"Mr Ar, you just can't do nothin' with a guy like Pyne! You can't try any reforming nonsense on him."

"No reform for Harry Pyne," agreed Rollison. "He's a hundred per center, and we've got to face it. How many of this particular crowd is as bad, Bill?"

Ebbutt hesitated.

"They aren't all bad kids," Wrightson conceded. "Not all of them, by a long chalk. There are some who're neely as bad as Pyne, though."

"Just what are you trying to do, Mr Ar?" Ebbutt demanded, stubbornly, and he reminded Rollison very much of Jolly in his manner, although it was like comparing a rogue elephant with an elderly fox.

"I suppose I'm trying to draw their teeth," Rollison said reflectively.

"You mind they don't use theirs to tear you apart," said Ebbutt. "I've heard one or two stories about what happened at that caff this afternoon. And I heard a whisper that Pyne's got a little armoury of knives and things that you wouldn't like tried out on yourself, Mr Ar."

Rollison said softly: "Where does he keep it?"

"At his flat, above the caff."

"That's useful to know," said Rollison. "Bill, thanks for your help and don't worry." He took the envelopes and slipped some into his coat pockets and some into his hip pocket, then went on: "Can you lend me a bike?"

"I daresay," said Ebbutt, glumly.

"Cheer up, Bill," urged Rollison. "Still keep a barrel of 4 XXXX here?"

"Same as I keep me thirst," Ebbutt said, more cheerfully.

"I've never been more thirsty, either," Rollison said, and sounded as if he meant it. "Ever heard of a secret way out of the Whale Street Club, Bill?"

Ebbutt and Wrightson had heard rumours, they agreed, and it was a common boast among the Slobs that they could get out of the Club at very short notice if there was a police raid, but Ebbutt had no idea where the secret exit was.

Rollison left the gymnasium a little before eleven o'clock, and he knew that Ebbutt and Wrightson were watching. He cycled off into the darkness and the dimness of the mean streets, with the envelopes containing the cards placed in the best order for delivering from Ebbutt's gymnasium; and he knew the East End so well that he did not have to refer to a map or to ask for directions. He cycled to house after house, most of them tiny, although about a dozen members of the Slob Mob lived in blocks of flats. He was seen by at least half a dozen people, slipping the envelopes into the letter boxes, and he made no attempt to hide himself. The delivery of sixty-two messages took him nearly three hours, and in the early hours of the morning he turned into Gresham Terrace on the bicycle, watched by a policeman in uniform, who came walking steadily towards him, obviously believing that he had discovered a would-be burglar. Rollison waited for him, and the policeman said:

"Mind telling me what you're doing here?"

Rollison said in his natural speaking voice: "That's the way to talk to the suspect! Thanks, officer. I've been out to a fancy dress party."

"Mr Rollison!"

"I'm afraid so," said Rollison. "Will it be all right if I stand my bike against the curb underneath this lamp?"

"Don't see why not, sir," the constable said. He stared from Rollison to the cycle, and began to chuckle. "Didn't expect I'd ever live to see you on a bike, sir! Bit hard on the old muscles, isn't it?"

"Very hard," Rollison agreed earnestly. He smiled, proffered cigarettes, then entered the quiet house and went up the stairs.

The green light went on, and Jolly opened the door; he was in a dressing-gown and slippers, and looked very tired. Rollison wished there was some way of making sure that his man would never wait up for him; but probably Jolly had been so worried that he hadn't been able to sleep. Ebbutt's mood was much the same. It was a harrassing thought, for although both men had been worried about him before, it had never been at this stage in an affair. Everything they said and did, as well as all that Nicholson had said and Grice appeared to think, suggested that all of them believed that he was slowing down; that he could no longer hope to have the speed or the alertness to overcome the Slob Mob. Why did they think that? He certainly did not feel he had lost speed, but was a man the best judge of himself? He had never seriously wondered about this before, and didn't much like the self-interrogation. But it was half past two, he was tired and was soon half asleep. Almost his last waking thought was to wonder what Harry Pyne would say in the morning.

* * *

Pyne did not get a great deal of post, although every week three different football pools organisers sent him coupons, and a few advertisements for racing tipsters and notices about boxing and wrestling came his way. Occasionally, too, there was a card from one of the Slob Mob. This particular morning, the Pools coupons were there together with a manilla-coloured envelope which was sealed, and addressed on an old typewriter in purple ink. Pyne noticed that there was no stamp. He picked the envelope up, slowly, and stared down at it. He had not really recovered from the shocks yesterday evening, nor had he recovered from the way Ginger had asserted his own authority to stop the quarrel with Girodo. He wasn't yet sure whether Girodo knew anything about the Toff's cards, but had decided not to risk an open clash with Ginger.

Ginger was going down well with the Mob, and it was probably a good thing to let him have his head occasionally—if the Mob thought he was really the leader, not simply the leader in name, it could be a very valuable asset.

Pyne moved across the room and pulled the stereophonic record player from the wall. Behind it was a little cupboard, built in the wall, and once used to house electric and gas meters which were now outside on the landing; he did not like his privacy invaded by anyone without his express invitation. The cupboard was an excellent hiding place and repository, and inside it were his weapons.

He unlocked the door.

It was nearly nine o'clock, and broad daylight. The sun caught a corner of the window, and touched the brightness of a knife blade as he moved it, reflecting in his eyes, and dazzling him. There were two lengths of bicycle chain, a small metal ball with two spikes on it, fastened to a chain, two packets of double edged razor blades, a pair of knuckle dusters, and two whips, made with barbed wire instead of leather or cord. Possession of such a collection was itself enough to earn a man several years in jail.

Pyne, who had found himself thinking of the weapons at the same time as he was thinking of Rollison, picked up a very thin-bladed stiletto-like knife. When he pressed a catch, the blade disappeared into the handle. He pressed again, and the blade stabbed out. He used it as a paper knife, slit open the envelope, hesitated, and then shook the contents out on to his hand. He did so very deliberately and slowly. He saw the corner of the card without showing any surprise; it had been obvious from the beginning that a small card was in here. Hard-faced, hard-eyed, he picked at the corner and drew it out.

He clenched his teeth when he saw the drawing, but did not lose his temper. He turned the card over, to the side which was the ordinary visiting card of the *Hon. Richard Rollison, 22g, Gresham Terrace, London, W.1.* He held it tightly, went to the cupboard again, took a razor blade out of a new pack, and then began to slice the card, so that tiny white strips fell to the floor. He cut it until there was only a small triangular piece left between his thumb and finger. He let this fall.

As he did so, he heard footsteps thudding on the stairs from the café. He watched the door, narrow-eyed. Two men were coming in wild haste, and he winced as one of them thumped on the door.

Ginger called out: "Harry, I got to see you!"

Harry Pyne said: "Wait a minute." He put the flick knife into his pocket, tucked the other weapons away and relocked the double doors of the little cupboard. Ginger was talking to someone else, impatiently, and when Pyne opened the door, Ginger and Smith were standing outside together, excitement blazing in their eyes, and each holding one of the Toff's cards.

"Take a dekko at this, Harry!" Ginger exclaimed. "Mine was in the letter box this morning, and Smithy had one, too. They've got one downstairs, Timmy Clark and Dusty've had them, it looks to me as if all the Mob's had a card from the Toff. What are we going to do about that?"

Pyne said stonily: "Any ideas?"

"We can't take it laying down," Ginger said, hotly. "My God, I'll teach him!"

"We aren't going to take it laying down," said Harry Pyne. He wiped a beading of sweat off his forehead, and went on: "He couldn't have taken these round by himself, so we've got to find out who helped him. I know who I think it was—that Ebbutt crowd." He hesitated, and then went on thinly: "But we'd better be sure before we teach them a lesson. Smithy, you find as many of the boys as you can, and ask them if they saw anyone last night. Ginger, how about doing the same?"

"Tell you what," said Ginger King. "Just pass the word around that I said it's got to be laid on. Okay? Be some time before we can check everyone, half the Mob won't be out of work until five or six tonight, but we can make a start. Fix it, Harry."

Pyne looked at him through his lashes, and said very slowly and as if reluctantly:

"Sure, I'll fix it."

Ginger nodded, taking acquiescence for granted.

17

MARKING TIME?

By the middle of that afternoon, nearly all of the East End, practically every policeman on the Metropolitan area, all of Ebbutt's friends and many of Rollison's, as well as most of the Chelham and district students, had some idea of what was going on. The story of the delivery of the cards to every member of the Slob Mob had got round—only two had been missed, not being on Ebbutt's list—but no one paid that omission much attention. The story had even spread to the newspapers. The *Evening Globe* handled it best: it gave a double enlargement of the man without a face, and a smaller picture of the normal side of the card, and beneath was the caption:

WE TIP THE TOFF TO WIN

Ebbutt's men, doing their best to make sure that the East End grape-vine carried every message, heard of the intensive questioning among the Slob Mob, and friends and relatives of the Mob. By half past seven on the evening after his cycle ride, they reported to Rollison that Ginger King and Pyne now knew that one man had distributed the cards.

"Most of the Mob reckons it was you in person, Mr Ar," said Ebbutt, "but Pyne won't have it."

"Sure of that, Bill?"

"Positive," said Ebbutt. "I don't know what to think, and that's the truth. You got some of the Mob in two minds, Mr Ar, if it wasn't for Pyne I'd say you're on a winner. But I don't think Pyne will let you win, though."

"Thanks, Bill," Rollison said. "Keep me informed right up to the minute, won't you?"

He rang off, thinking ruefully that a year ago it would

not have occurred to Ebbutt that Pyne or anyone else could prevent the Toff from winning. Rollison pondered the more unpleasant and foreboding elements of this fact, and was stirred out of reflection by a ring at the front door bell. Jolly went to the door, and returned to announce without surprise that Nicholson had called.

"I'll see him," Rollison said. "He's probably come to tell me sinister things about *anno domini*."

Certainly nothing in Nicholson's manner or appearance suggested that he had relented, but he accepted whisky and water without hesitating, and when Jolly had served it and gone out of the room, he said solemnly:

"Your very good health, Mr Rollison, and I hope I will be able to say that to a live man a week from now."

"I'll drink to that, too," said Rollison, brightly, and drank deeply; Nicholson's manner more than his words needled him, but he showed no outward sign. "Aren't you very sanguine?"

"You really made Pyne mad, Mr Rollison. All the reports from the Division say the same thing—you've turned this into a personal feud." Nicholson eyed Rollison with his rather colourless and lifeless grey eyes as he went on almost as if talking to himself: "You always meant to, in spite of our advice, didn't you?"

"It seemed the only way of handling the situation," said Rollison. "I'll be careful, and I shall also stay alive."

"I hope so," Nicholson said, ponderously. "One thing's certain, Mr Rollison—Pyne won't miss a chance of getting you. And even if we were to pick him up as soon as he'd done for you, it wouldn't be much consolation to you, would it?"

"Very graphic," said Rollison.

"I have been considering the possibility of picking him up," announced Nicholson.

"I hope you'll forget that," said Rollison, quietly. "If we put off the issue any longer, I might get careless. At the moment I half expect him to jump out of your pocket. What could you pick him up for?"

"We haven't really got anything on him, but we could try loitering with intent, or—"

"If you pick him up and have to release him immediately afterwards for lack of evidence, you'll only make him a hero to the Mob," Rollison said. "That wouldn't help, would it?"

"I see your point."

"Thanks," said Rollison. "I shouldn't worry about me too much, either."

Nicholson finished his drink, put the glass down with a bang on the corner of Rollison's big desk, looked long at the hangman's rope, then from it towards as ugly an assortment of knives, daggers, and razor blades as there was at the Black Museum, and said very deliberately:

"But we do worry, Mr Rollison, we really do. Well, I must be going. Have you seen the evening newspapers?"

"That nonsense about my card?"

"Not nonsense of any kind," said Nicholson. "Young Alec Price is on the danger list."

"Oh, is he," said Rollison, heavily.

"His parents are at the hospital. They've rushed here from Manchester," went on Nicholson. "It will be a very bad thing if the boy dies. Have you seen any of his friends?"

"Not today," said Rollison. "I couldn't be more sorry."

As soon as Nicholson had left, Jolly served dinner, but Rollison's appetite was nothing like so good as it had been before Nicholson had brought his news and his gloom. So it was less important when, half way through the meal, the telephone bell rang. Rollison had an extension plugged in close to the dining-table, and leaned to one side so as to take the call.

"Rollison here."

"Mr Rollison," said Doris Evans. "I think I ought to tell you that I can't do any more with Jonas. If Alec should die—"

"Who said anything about dying?" Rollison was sharp.

"Well, the news isn't very encouraging, is it?" said

Doris flatly. "Mr and Mrs Price are at his bedside, and Jonas hasn't been allowed to see him today." She paused; and when she went on, it was in a more hurried voice. "I wondered if you would come round and see Jonas."

"Yes, I will," said Rollison promptly. "Where is he?"

"We'll be at my flat."

"I'll be there in half-an-hour," promised Rollison, and put down the receiver.

Jolly had heard the last remark, came in and took away a plate still half full of pheasant, game chips, and mushrooms, and substituted a lemon mousse and whipped cream. Rollison had a couple of spoonsful, and pushed his chair back. He was on the way to the door when he heard footsteps approaching outside, and remembered the time when the two youths with bicycle chains had been waiting on the landing. He glanced up into the mirror, to see Ray Harrison; the newspaperman looked worried. Rollison opened the door as the bell rang, calling: "It's all right. Jolly." Harrison looked startled at the quick opening of the door, and backed away.

"I was just going out," Rollison said. "Can we talk in my car?"

"Oh, sure," said Harrison, at once. "Anywhere will do."

"All right, Jolly," Rollison said again as his man came to the door. "I'll telephone you if I expect to be late." He saw Jolly watching the newspaperman closely and suspected that Jolly wondered whether Harrison was bringing news of any impending attack; if he were, it was surely better that Jolly should not know. Rollison went downstairs by the *Evening Globe* man's side, quite sure that Harrison was unhappy and disturbed. They reached the street, where Rollison's sand-and-blue Bentley stood glowing in the street lamplight. The Jaguar had been returned to its garage in St John's Wood.

Near the Bentley was a taxi.

"I'll pay my cab off," said Harrison, and as Rollison got into the Bentley and started the engine, he went over to the taxi-driver. He came hurrying back, and climbed in next to Rollison, asking: "Where are you going?"

"To see Doris Evans."

"I wondered if you would," said Harrison. "See that piece in the *Evening Globe*? We picked up one of your cards from one of the Slobs, for the photograph."

"Very smart," Rollison said.

"Rolly," said Harrison heavily, "I wish to God I hadn't become involved in this. It's gone much further than I expected. We've got contacts all over the East End—you know that, don't you?"

"And several of them have telephoned you to say that Pyne is going to get the Toff at all costs."

"That's it," said Harrison. "That's absolutely it, except for one thing."

"What's that?"

"He means it."

"He seems to me as if he's talking too much to be a man of action."

"If I could get you out of London for the next couple of weeks, I would," declared Harrison. "I've just been out to see Bill Ebbutt, and to compare notes. He's got much the same story. Pyne and Ginger King have taken the attitude that it's curtains for the Toff or curtains for them."

"Yes," Rollison said, and forced a chuckle. "So I gathered. Ray, I am not scared of a gang of young hoodlums, now or at any time. Tell Bill Ebbutt that, will you?"

Harrison said: "Rolly."

"Yes?"

"The rumour is that they're not going to kill you."

"Obliging of them," murmured Rollison.

"Don't be so blasted flippant," rasped Harrison angrily. "I'm serious. They say that they're going to cut you up so that plastic surgery won't be any help. They want you to be a living wreck so that they can tell the rest of the world how clever they are—but there won't be any risk of the death penalty for them."

"Ah," said Rollison. "The idea's been thought of before—"

"Rolly, for God's sake, listen to me! You've riled Pyne so that he can't think of anything but getting you. Everything we know about him shows that he's quite capable of doing what he plans to do. You'll be crazy if you don't listen."

"I'm sure, I will," said Rollison, and after a pause he added: "Can I drop you anywhere?"

Harrison growled: "Anywhere I can get a cab will do."

Rollison dropped the newspaperman in Buckingham Palace Road, and drove on through the twisting streets between Victoria and Sloane Square, then along Fulham Road, and finally to the street where Doris Evans and Anne Darby lived. He saw three small cars drawn up near the house, five motor scooters, and two motor-cycles. As he pulled up behind a scooter, a youth appeared from a doorway, much as one had two nights ago, and called:

"Mr Rollison?"

"Yes."

"Thanks for coming," the youth said fervently. "It's straight up the stairs to the top of the house. They're expecting you, you won't have to knock."

Rollison went in. Compared with houses in the East End or the near-derelict quarters of London, this was a palace. The walls had recently been papered and the paintwork was fresh, while there was some carpet on the floor, quite bright and cheerful. As he neared the third and top landing, he heard voices, then saw a girl's face at an open door. She didn't see him at first, and he heard Jonas Lee's voice:

"I don't care what you say, I'm going to fix those swine."

"But Jonas, you'll only make things worse." That was Anne Darby, and there seemed to be a scared note in her voice. "It isn't any use—"

"There's only one way of dealing with a mob like that,"

said Jonas, "and that's to let them feel the thick end of
your fist. If Alec dies——"

He broke off, as if the thought was too dreadful to con-
template. Rollison moved up two more steps and the
girl at the door exclaimed: "Here's the Toff!" Rollison
smiled at her and went to the door which she opened
wide. The room beyond was unexpectedly large. Two
divan beds were close against the wall at either side,
leaving ample room in the middle for a table, easy chairs
and an old-fashioned sofa. In one corner was a small television set, next to a portable record player. At least a
dozen youths sat about the room, two youths to every
girl. The centre of attention was Jonas Lee, of course, with
Doris—who was sitting on a pouffe, cross-legged, while
Jonas stood with his back to the window. He looked very
small and absurdly young, but there was no doubt of his
physical strength or his courage. He waited for the Toff
to draw closer to him. Most of the youths jumped to their
feet, and all of them watched Rollison very closely. It
was easy to sense that most of them were on Doris's side,
as easy to see that two or three of the men obviously sided
with the young Australian. That showed in the way they
glared at Rollison, in their attitude of defiance.

Jonas said: "I don't mean any disrespect, Mr Rollison,
but no one can stop me, not even you. I'm going to raid
the Slob Mob's place again tonight even if I have to go
alone."

"If Alec dies," Rollison said, quietly, "I'll come with
you."

18

PROMISE

THE silence which followed Rollison's words affected everyone; a dozen pairs of eyes were turned towards him, none of them steadier than Jonas Lee's. Anne Darby moved before any of the others, and sidled to Jonas's side; for the first time it dawned on Rollison that she was nearly as strong a character as Jonas. Now they faced him with mingled doubt, defiance, and hopefulness, and it was obvious that Jonas did not believe what Rollison had said.

"You mean that?" Anne asked.

"Yes."

"Is it a promise?"

Careful not to smile at her naiveté, Rollison said: "Yes, it is."

"Jonas," said Anne. "Mr Rollison says he will come with you."

After a long pause, Jonas said: "Good-o."

"You don't sound exactly enthusiastic," Rollison remarked.

"Don't I?" asked Jonas. He glanced down at his hands, and there was a strapping of plaster and gauze over the knuckles of his left; he picked at the tape with his nail. "Let's have it straight, Mr Rollison. If Alec dies I'm going to raid Whale Street, and as true as I'm here I'm going to pull that Club to pieces. If I get my hands on any of the Slob Mob, I'll tear them apart."

"I know exactly what you mean."

"And you'll come with me?"

"I'll come with you."

Slowly, Jonas began to smile. His babyish face took on an even younger look, his teeth showed a brilliant white, and he looked as if for the moment he had thrown away doubts and fear.

"Good-o!" he said explosively. "If you come, that'll bring all the others. How about that, Anne?" He slid his arm round Anne's tiny waist, and gave her a hug which seemed to drive the breath out of her body. "Thanks, Mr Rollison, I knew we could rely on you."

Only Doris seemed to be puzzled, Rollison thought; perhaps only Doris really understood that it would be impossible to stop Jonas, except by holding him back by force, and that the one way of avoiding a disastrous clash between the two groups was to go with the Chelham students and cool their ardour. To Rollison the most important immediate task was to ease the present tension; judging from the expressions on the faces of all the youngsters, he had succeeded. He tried to compare these teenagers with the Slob Mob. Give them different clothes and slightly longer and dirtier hair, and there wouldn't really be all that difference; the one characteristic of both groups was their youth, their obvious health, and their vitality. They were bursting for action. He wondered whether there was any way of bringing both sides together in amity, and put the thought out of his mind. At the moment he had to get Jonas and the others with him.

He said casually: "I've been trying to stir the Slob Mob up."

"That so?" asked Jonas. "How?"

Rollison put his hand to his pocket, and flicked one of his cards across. With a speed which was almost sleight of hand, Jonas trapped it against his chest; and then he amused and yet puzzled Rollison by ignoring it. Instead, he grinned and said:

"Visiting card?"

"Did you hear about that?"

"Sure we did," said Jonas. "We had a visit from some newspaper fella, name of Harrison. Smart idea, Mr Rollison." There was a lack of spirit in the comment, a kind of forced heartiness which puzzled Rollison even more; he did not think Jonas Lee was as simple and easy to understand as he made out. Everyone else with the exception of Doris now seemed to be relaxed and even contented; they were so very young, Rollison thought—and with a sense almost of shock he realised that when they looked at him they would have the same thought in reverse; the thought that Grice and Nicholson, Jolly and Harrison, had already put into his mind in several different ways. Jonas might well be thinking: "*He's a nice guy, but he's past it.*" Everything Rollison had heard, all the warnings and the talk of menace, suggested that the Slob Mob did not share that view, but if Jonas and his friends did, how much did it matter whether he went with them or not?

"Sure I heard about it," Jonas said. "We wished you'd used us as messenger boys, Mr Rollison—most folks agree we can do that kind of job very well. What was the idea?"

"Do I have to tell you, Jonas?"

"Sure. Tell us all," said Jonas, and the youngster's manner made Rollison feel even more uneasy.

Rollison said: "The card could make the Slob Mob mad, and angry people get careless."

"Good tactics," praised Jonas, airily, and looked round at his lieutenants. "How about a can of beer?" he demanded with forced heartiness, and stabbed a finger at one of the youths, who jumped up at once. Two others did the same, and Rollison noticed the authority which Jonas had over them; this, in its way, was a leadership as positive as Harry Pyne's, certainly more positive than Ginger King's.

The three youths came back from the kitchen carrying bottles of beer, pewter tankards, and some thick glasses. Quite suddenly the whole group became talkative, almost merry. Rollison took a tankard and squatted on a pouffe near Anne, watching young Jonas covertly. Doris came across to him and sat on a pouffe close by, then put her right hand into his and began to stroke it gently with her fingers; would he ever be able to understand the girl? Wasn't it a fact that he could not really understand these youngsters at all? He could only understand those with the quality of evil when he recognised it.

Or was he under-estimating himself? Wasn't this crowd as basically simple, even basically the same, as the Slob Mob?

He wondered what would happen if Alec Price died, and did not like reflecting on the fact that the life or death of an eighteen-year-old youth would make all the difference to what was going to happen in the next few hours. If Alec pulled through, then reason would have a chance; if he died—

One of the youngsters, near the window, suddenly jumped to his feet and raised his right hand. The others fell silent, as if they were used to this kind of signal. The youngster went close to the window, as a motor-cycle engine clattered, then fell away into silence.

"Who is it?" asked Jonas.

The other youth pressed his face close to the window, and announced:

"Charley."

"Who—" began Rollison, and Doris squeezed his hand very tightly, as if she were warning him not to ask questions; but the answers to unspoken questions were already hovering in the air. The sudden quiet; the tension; the way that one youth strode to the door to open it. Footsteps sounded, quite clear and distinct in spite of the stair carpet.

Doris whispered: "He's the hospital scout."

"Oh," Rollison whispered back.

Someone had been at the hospital, then, to bring news of Alec Price. Judging from the attitude of all of those here, they expected this news to be bad. Rollison felt his own pulse beating very fast, had to force himself to keep still and to keep quiet.

The footsteps were on the landing outside. Jonas Lee stood with his arm round Anne Darby's waist, watching the open door. His lips were parted in a set smile, his hands were clenched—the one at Anne's waist seemed very tiny.

A small, shock-haired youth came in. He had a narrow

face and a wriggly nose and a pair of glittering dark eyes. He stood in the doorway for a moment, as if fully aware of the dramatic situation he was creating; then in a simple, single gesture, he told them all the worst.

He poked his thumb towards the floor.

Everyone there except the Toff drew in a hissing breath. Jonas said: "Is he dead?"

"Yes."

"When?"

"Just before I left. I fixed it with the porter to find out, he had a grapevine leading to the nurses' room." The boy was trying to be so bold and blasé, but tears in his eyes shimmered on them in the light; he had lived alone with death for as long as it had taken him to come from the hospital. He gulped, and had difficulty in finishing: "It's curtains all right."

"So Alec's dead, and they killed him," Jonas said. He looked across at Rollison. His eyes glittered, his teeth seemed to glint in the poor light above his head. "They murdered him," he repeated. "Okay, Charley. Get everyone tipped off. You know where to meet."

Rollison said: "Where?"

"We've got it all laid on, Toff," said Jonas, in a very formal voice. "We knew we would have to have a plan all ready to put into action, this wasn't a job we could improvise. Took a leaf out of your book, see—always be prepared. The chaps have been given their orders. They'll go by different routes to Tower Hill, and we've got a couple of coaches laid on to take us from there to Whale Street. It's all fixed, Toff."

"Then let's go," said Rollison, and stood up briskly. Doris's fingers seemed to be biting into his flesh, painfully.

"Right," said Jonas, and waited for the Toff as the other youths went crowding towards the door.

What followed seemed inevitable to the Toff from the moment it began to happen, but not until it was too late to save himself. One moment, he was moving towards Jonas

Lee, the next Jonas drove his clenched right fist to Rollison's chin. He did it on the turn, his elbow bent, a hook-punch delivered with all his strength behind it. Rollison had time only to raise his right arm to try to fend the blow off, but it was far too late. He felt the agonising pain, his body seemed to scream as the blood was drawn towards the nerve centre. He saw Jonas's face going round and round, he felt his knees bending, he heard sounds which might have been screams, might have been imaginary, might have been the screeching of brakes or the screaming of an express train. He hit the floor. He felt two more blows, one to his chin, one to the back of his neck. Had these been body blows they would not have mattered; it was almost as if Jonas knew that it would be a waste of time attacking the body.

Rollison did not lose consciousness, but for the moment he lay still, dazed, anxious not to encourage any further attack.

* * *

"Jonas!" screamed Doris, as Rollison fell.

"Forget it, Dorry," Jonas Lee said. "Old pal Toff didn't mean what he said. He wouldn't have done anything to help, and you know it. He would have come to try to calm us down, that's all. Now don't you—"

"You silly idiot!" Doris cried. "He's worth ten of you, he knows more about the Slob Mob than all of us put together. If you don't take his advice—"

"Alec's dead, remember?" Jonas said, icily. "He used to be a friend of yours."

"Jonas, listen to me," Doris pleaded. "You'll only run into trouble, you won't help Alec this way. You've got to wait for the Toff to—"

"Sorry, ducky," said Jonas. "No wait." He glanced behind her, and for the first time she realised that one of the other youths was there; and as she jumped forward, her arms were pinioned to her sides.

"If you keep still this won't hurt," Jonas went on. "But we can't trust you or the Toff not to phone the police."

"*What are you going to do?*" gasped Doris.

"Take a leaf out of the Toff's book," Jonas declared—and then Doris felt something soft brush over her face; another youth was behind her, holding a woollen scarf. Before Doris could cry out again, the scarf was pulled tightly over her mouth, gagging her.

As swiftly, another youth pulled her arms behind her, and tied her wrists together behind her back.

Quite gently, Jonas lifted her off her feet and laid her full length on the floor in front of the couch, and one of the others tied her ankles together. She saw two youths bending over Rollison on the far side of the room; they were treating him in exactly the same way as they had her.

Jonas was over with Rollison, but soon he came back.

"Now put the light out," he ordered. "And lock them in."

Doris heard the footsteps, and then a click. A moment later the door closed with a snap, and she heard the key turn in the lock.

There was no sound at all from Rollison.

*　　*　　*

Rollison was aware of everything that happened, and desperately anxious because the surprise attack had been so effective. He realised when Doris was being treated in the same way, he felt the cloth over his mouth, first, then the hurried tugging at his arms, so that they could be tied behind him. It would not take long for Jonas Lee and his cronies to get to Whale Street, and there was very little time.

He could see only one hope of stopping the disaster. He tensed his hands and his wrists as a youth grabbed them, and another wound a tie round them; a tie, which would give. The youth fastened the knot vigorously, and gave an extra pull, but did not realise that the wrists were flexed. When he had finished, he seemed satisfied, and Rollison heard him say:

"This okay, Jonas?"

"Let's see," said Jonas.

Rollison flexed his wrists and arms again, hoping desperately that Jonas would notice nothing wrong. He felt Jonas's fingers poking, and heard the youth say:

"Okay. Let's go."

When they had gone, Rollison let the tension relax; the tie was a little loose, but he hadn't much time in which to get his hands free; he wasn't absolutely sure that he could.

*   *   *

As Rollison and Doris lay in that flat, cyclists, motor-cyclists, and youths on motor-scooters left the street, and hurried to carry their message to the other Chelham students; all of the youths involved had been on the alert. On bicycles, crowded into small cars, in every kind of vehicle that could be pressed into service and would not be particularly noticeable, the students left the Chelham area and headed for the pre-arranged rendezvous at Tower Hill, where the Tower was floodlit so as to make the centuries merge—and where tourists were always likely to be, even as late as this. It was cleverly and cunningly done, for they all took different routes, even using different side streets, to make sure that there was no likelihood that the police would suspect what they were doing.

At Tower Hill, two motor coaches arranged by the brother of one of the students were waiting; here, the police would take little notice of them. Both coaches were marked LONDON BY NIGHT, SPECIAL TOUR. By ten o'clock, the first of the students had boarded a coach, and within ten minutes both coaches were full. There were, in all, eighty-seven students, some of them sitting three on a seat made for two. The drivers of the coaches knew exactly where to go. The police in the city area had no reason to believe that the coaches were not what the notices on them claimed: touring parties of all age groups often went into the East End at night, to visit one or two of the famous river pubs, to get a vicarious thrill out of what had once been Chinatown and was still called Limehouse, and to see ships loading at night.

No police reported what was happening because none believed that it was worth reporting.

19

COUNTER-PLOT

About the time that Rollison reached the Chelham flat and began to talk to Jonas Lee, Harry Pyne, Ginger, Smith, and one other member of the Slob Mob went to the Whale Street Club. The police were watching from several vantage points, but no action would be taken if only a few of the Mob went to the club premises, and Pyne judged police reactions carefully and had not miscalculated. He actually tipped his hat at one policeman who was standing at a corner near the stage door entrance. Pyne knew that a second Divisional man was hiding in the shadows nearby; they hoped that if only one was seen, it might provoke some kind of attack and give an excuse for holding him, Harry, or any member of the Mob.

None of them made a false move.

They went to a small room which led off the main dance hall, and sat round a table, much as they had at the flat above Girodo's Café. Pyne had said very little since the clash with Ginger about the Toff's cards, and in a way he was relieved to find the others took his advice and met together. This room was used as an office, although very little office work was done in it. A single telephone stood on a small table, near Pyne's right hand. He pushed a packet of cigarettes across the table, and looked at Ginger.

"Okay, Ginger?"

"Why shouldn't I be?"

"I just wondered," Pyne said. "Ginger, you know what's going to happen if that guy Price kicks the bucket."

Ginger said: "I can guess."

"The police—" began Smith, uneasily.

"Forget the cops, we can deal with the cops," said Pyne, harshly.

"But they could call it murder."

"You're crazy," Pyne said. "They couldn't even call it manslaughter; it was an accident. Price fell down and hit his head—so what. They don't know who did it—"

"You're forgetting something," Smith objected. He ran his hand over his round head, as if he were feeling the bumps to find one as painful and as dangerous as the one on Alec Price's head. His face looked rather like a turnip, with big round eyes cut out, and a little button of a nose stuck on. There was no doubt that he was scared.

"I don't forget nothing," Pyne said.

"You're forgetting that Luigi and me was booked for that raid on the Toff's flat!"

"Forget it," Pyne sneered. "You were in the flat when Price got his, weren't you? There's only one of us in trouble and that's Micky Herrin, but Micky was looking after that girl, he could prove he didn't have anything to do with hitting Price or knocking him down. The cops don't know the names of the rest of the boys who were at the Toff's place. You chicken?"

"I'm not chicken, but—"

"No one's chicken," Ginger King interrupted, sharply. "Smiffy, we'll duck out from any murder rap. You don't have to worry."

Harry gave a grudging smile: "Thanks, Ginger," he said. "You've got it right on the knob. We can deal with the cops, if Price dies, but his pals will be here as soon as you can say knife."

"How can you be sure?" Smith demanded.

"Like to bet?"

"Harry's right again," Ginger put in, with an authority which obviously impressed Smith and the other man, who had made no comment. "They'll swarm round the place like flies, don't you worry."

"So what will we do?" demanded Smith.

Pyne said, very slowly: "I'll tell you what we ought to do, Smiffy. We ought to make flickin' fools of them. We ought to let them come and take over the Club and then we'll lock the buzzards in." He was watching Ginger as he spoke, obviously anxious to judge Ginger's reaction, and after the first moment of startled surprise, Ginger began to grin. Pyne smiled secretively to himself, but there was nothing pleasant about his expression.

"I don't get it," Smith said.

"Listen, bird brain," Pyne jeered. "They come spoiling for a fight, see. Who wants a fight right now? We've got plenty on our hands, we don't want to get the raw edge of the law, do we? Who wants trouble for the sake of trouble? We want to show the cops that we're anxious not to have a fight—that right, Ginger?"

"Harry Boy," said Ginger warmly, "you're making a lot of sense."

"I'm making sense," Harry Pyne agreed, with smug confidence. "So this is what we do. We leave a few of the Mob here, see, to act as bait. We have the lights on, same as usual. When these Chelham so-and-so's come, they'll see the light and think we're all on the premises. We can have the record-player on—"

"Harry, that's real bright, that is," Ginger applauded, and grinned even more broadly. "Sure, we have the record player on, so they think we're dancing."

"So they raid us," Harry went on. "The way I would do it, I would have two or three boyos at the side entrance —so that's what the Chelham mob will do. They'll have three, say, or four or maybe five at the side entrance, planning to catch us if we start running. That's what they'll do, and that's what they'll think, but when they're inside we'll lock 'em in—we can double bar the front doors, like they used to be barred, and block the porch with a car. We can put the shutters up at the windows, too, that won't take long. All we've got to worry about is making sure that the party they send round the side way can't let them out. So—"

"How are you going to fix that?" demanded Smith, still dubiously.

"I've been thinking about that," said Pyne. "You know how narrow the street is along there—just room for one car and a coupla feet of pavement. So this is what we do: as soon as they've come, we turn a van over across the end of the street. It's as simple as that. The street's so narrow, they'll be trapped, and they won't be able to get out of the windows or the front door, either. It's dead easy."

He looked at Ginger for approval.

"Harry boy," agreed Ginger, happily, "it's dead easy. But there's one little thing you've forgotten, old pal."

"What's that, Ginger?"

"They've got a friend, haven't they?" inquired Ginger, with exaggerated innocence. "Their good old friend, counsellor, and guide, don't they call him?"

Pyne began to smile.

"You couldn't mean Mr Toff Rollison, old boy, could you?"

"No, bai Jove, I couldn't, could I?" demanded Ginger, and then he thumped the table with the flat of his hand. "I mean the bloody Toff, that's exactly who I mean! Think he'll come with them?"

"If he comes with them, it's okay," said Pyne. "If he stays away, it's okay, too. Because when the Chelham gang's shut up here, who's going to worry about Rollison? We can deal with Rollison nice and quietly, and take our time. But if you ask me," went on Pyne, "he'll come with the Chelham crowd all right. I've been studying *Mister* Rollison's record, and I reckon I can see the way his mind works. He'll come with them to try to cool them down, and we'll have a special card of welcome ready for the Toff, that's what we'll have. Okay, Ginger?"

"I couldn't have said it better myself," Ginger assured him warmly. He slapped the table again, and then guffawed. In the middle of the laugh, the telephone bell rang. He was still laughing when Pyne plucked the receiver up, and still laughing when Pyne exclaimed:

"What's that?"

He listened intently; and Ginger fell silent, while Smith and the man who had not yet spoken watched narrow-eyed.

"So he's dead," Pyne said into the telephone. He gave a
sigh that was almost one of relief. "Okay, Pete, that's the
signal. How about the Chelham mob? . . . Sure, I know
. . . Sure, it's my opinion they'll head this way—*what's*
that?" Pyne seemed to hold the receiver more tightly and
his whole body seemed to go tense; then he began to
smile as if with absolute delight. "So he is," he said. "So
he is. Okay, Pete, keep us posted."

Pyne replaced the receiver, and then rubbed his hands
together very slowly, as if he were trying to keep the
others in suspense. But at last he said succinctly:

"Price is a goner, that's a fact. Rollison's with that
Aussie flicker, right now, and the whole crowd's on the
move. We'd better get ready, boyos. And when we start,
let me tell you something. We want to make the cop, believe we're packing this place up, that's why we're shutting
up the Club. That all clear? Smiffy, you and Decker can
talk about it as you go out, maybe you can be having a
moan and saying you don't see the sense in it. That
okay?"

"Suits me," said Smith. "S'easy."

Three different police constables from the Division
heard Smith, Pyne, and Ginger King comment sourly on
the fact that they were going to change their headquarters,
so it occasioned no unusual comment when some of the
members of the Slob Mob began to close the big steel
shutters, fitted inside the windows. These had been placed
there many years ago, as a defence against bomb splinter
damage, when the Whale Street Club had been in use as a
Civil Defence Centre. The shutters were all reinforced
with iron slats, and there were slats which fitted into the
front doors, too. There was nothing surprising in the fact
that the music was on in the dance room all the time,
either, for the Slob Mob was notoriously music crazy. Nor
was there anything surprising in the fact that they left the
side door open; they had to have some way of getting in
and out, and that was the obvious one.

Reports to the Divisional Police Station were passed on

to Nicholson, of the Yard, who had learned that Price was dead, and who had sent out a warning for the police to be extra careful. He himself was preparing a case against Pyne and others of the gang, but it wasn't yet complete. When he heard that the Slob Mob was going to shut the Club, he was puzzled at first, but it was not long before the views of the Divisional men began to satisfy him. Very simply, they thought that the Slob Mob realised that the situation was too hot for them, and were going to change their headquarters in the hope of making the police believe they were turning over a new leaf.

"Take it from me, Nick," said the Divisional Superintendent, "it's only a stall. They'll go somewhere else or they'll be back as soon as this has blown over. Right now they're all scared because the death of Price might mean a murder rap for some of them, and they're going to tread very carefully. That man Pyne is up to all the tricks."

Nicholson said: "I hope so. Any news from Chelham?"

"Yes," said the D.S. "I just had a report from the Divisional HQ over there. The Chelham students have packed it in. They were told about Price's death, and it knocked the stuffing out of them. Instead of getting together in a big indignation party, they've gone crawling off home with their tails between their legs. You can take it from me there won't be any trouble from Chelham, now. They're not the real tough type. Price's death will have scared 'em."

Nicholson said: "I hope you're right, but I wouldn't like to put money on it. They laid on that protest march pretty cleverly, didn't they?"

"Come off it, Nick. We didn't have any idea what they were planning then, it was just a big joke. It's not so much of a joke any longer. We won't have any trouble from Chelham, and even if we should it won't take us long to deal with it. Compared with the Slob Mob, they're as soft as butter. You can go and have your beauty sleep, there's nothing to worry about here."

"I'll have a cuppa char for a start," said Nicholson, who

lost his prosiness when he was with his own colleagues. "Then I'll go along and have a look at the Whale Street Club, just for the sake of it."

"Sticker for duty, poor old Nick," said the D.S. "Look in when you're in this part of the world, won't you? I don't want it to seem as if the Yard's taken over my manor."

"I'll look in," Nicholson promised. "Heard anything more of Rollison?"

The D.S. laughed.

"Percy Bligh at Chelham told me he'd gone to see that young Aussie, Jonas Lee. If you ask me, Rollison cooled 'em down. Cunning old buzzard, our Toff. His card trick got the Pyne mob on the hop, too. The truth is, Nick, mobs like the Slob Mob aren't so tough as they used to be. The whole country's going soft."

"Could be," Nicholson conceded, but he was uneasy enough to telephone Rollison's flat, and even more uneasy when he learned that Rollison had not returned from Chelham. He was hungry, went down to the canteen, and was eating when the two coach loads of 'sightseers' started off from Tower Hill. Police observed this move, also, but none of them had seen any of the Chelham students before, and there was no reason at all to suspect the truth about these coach loads, especially as each started off towards the Tower Bridge, some distance from the heart of the East End. It was not until the coaches crossed the bridge that they put on speed, heading for the Rotherhithe Tunnel. Any driver who knew the road well could take them to the Whale Street area within fifteen minutes, and the driver of the first coach certainly knew the way. Going through the tunnel the thunderous noise seemed to heighten the expectancy among the youths.

The first warning of trouble came when two of the policemen on duty near Whale Street—who had turned in their reports, by telephone, about the closing of the Club— saw the coaches pass by the street lamps. It was not usual for sightseeing parties to come this way, and hardly likely that anyone would take a wrong turning. One of the policemen went towards the coach, as it slowed down; the other kept a wary eye from a distance, and touched the chain of his whistle, to make sure that it would come out quickly if he needed it. The coach came to a standstill very close to the side street, and as it did so, front door and emergency rear door opened, and youths poured out. They were all wearing rubber shoes, making little noise, and carried sticks or hammers, or pieces of knotted rope in their hands. The policeman nearer the coach called out in alarm:

"Whistle up, Tom!" and dropped his hand to his truncheon, shouting: "That's enough of that! Get back in the coach!" The policeman behind him snatched out his whistle and put it to his lips, but before he could blow, a youth hidden in the shadows, one of the Slob Mob, flung a half brick at his head and sent him lurching forward. He staggered, the whistle dangling from his pocket on its silvery chain, as the other policeman turned on his heel. Before this man could shout, whistle, or run, three of the youths from the Chelham coaches leapt at him. One flung a cloth over his head and tied it in a tight knot behind his neck, another fumbled at his waist-band for a pair of handcuffs, snatched them out, and locked the policeman's hands behind him. Then they hooked his feet from under him, saved him from falling heavily, and left him lying on the pavement huddled against the wall.

The youths from Chelham began to storm the Whale Street Club, where the din of canned music was still very loud, but the noise of banging doors and smashing glass began to sound above it. The policeman who had gone down first lay unconscious against a car parked awkwardly in front of the main entrance. Suddenly, the roar of a car or van engine driven at furious speed drowned all other sounds. The van's sidelights showed small and dim as the vehicle was driven towards the narrow side street, where four of the youths from Chelham had gone.

Harry Pyne had anticipated their tactics perfectly.

The driver of the van swung it in a half circle, crashed it against the end of a car parked near the corner, and swung it round so that it blocked the end of the street. Immediately, other members of the Slob Mob rushed from their hiding places and six of them used iron bars as levers with which to overturn the van. They sent it crashing, then turned and ran, leaving the two helpless policemen and the side entrance party of the Chelham students trapped.

Harry Pyne himself dropped the bars into the slats across the front doors, and another Slob Mob man drove a second van, stolen like the first, into the front porch. It was now impossible for anyone to force their way out.

Footsteps sounded further and further away from the Whale Street Club. People nearby who heard the crash kept it to themselves. No one had any reason to suspect exactly what had happened.

Inside, Jonas Lee was tearing about the dance hall and the room like a madman, looking for Slob Mob members who were not there, rushing to the stairs, rushing at the doors, finding all the windows shuttered and barred. The eighty-odd students who had gone to wreak their vengeance were baffled and a little scared; there was no excitement in fighting the air, and there was not a single member of the Slob Mob in this building.

The disappointment was so acute that Jonas seemed to go crazy, but he retained enough self control to keep command. At the back of his mind and in the minds of all the others was the realisation that they had been tricked and trapped. There was frustration and anger but there was also that sense of fear.

The Slob Mob had expected them, so the Slob Mob would soon attack.

* * *

One of the students said, uneasily: "If the Toff was with us we might know what to expect."

"To hell with him," Jonas Lee growled. "Let's get out of here."

20

THE DEVIL IN HARRY PYNE

As the members of the Slob Mob ran away from the crashed vans, Harry Pyne stayed behind with two of them. Soft-footed, furtive figures darted in and out of doorways, along alleys and into side streets, to make sure that no one could see exactly where they went, for on top of their minds was fear that the police had followed the two coaches.

At one corner, Harry Pyne spoke to a fair-haired youth who looked as if he should be home in bed.

"Go to the caff, Sam, and tell Ginger I won't be long."

"Okay, Harry," the boy said, and he quickened his pace; somehow one always did on orders from Pyne.

Pyne listened to his padding footsteps, and realised exactly what was going to happen, because he had arranged this kind of thing often before. In ones and twos, the Slob Mob would go to Girodo's café, where half the youths and most of the girls had been all the evening. The newcomers would slip inside, some going in the back entrance so as to avoid being noticed if the police were watching closely—as they would be tonight. When the Divisional C.I.D. came round to the Club and discovered the trouble, everyone in Girodo's would have a sort of alibi. Those who had been there all the evening would swear that their friends had been there, too; it was the kind of mass alibi which no policeman would ever believe, but which a magistrate or a jury might have to.

Within twenty minutes all the Slob Mob would be out of danger, and Ginger King would be on top of the world.

Ginger needed working on, but that could come later; the Whale Street Club and the Chelham students needed working on first, and Pyne knew exactly how to do it. He was tensed up and excited, and his excitement was touched with disappointment because the Toff had not gone into

the club house. He wondered if the Chelham kids had
fooled Rollison, or whether he would turn up soon; it
might be necessary to deal with him in person, and Pyne's
lips tightened and his heart thumped at the prospect.

He went back towards the Club.

Two women were at the doorway of a house further
along Whale Street, able to see the upturned van, but
there was no noise, no sound of fighting, nothing to suggest that the police ought to be called; the women probably believed the incident would be best forgotten. A little
man in a wheel chair called out: "You hear something?"

"Just going to find out," Pyne called back. If he could
have gone into the main part of the club building, he
could have avoided being seen, but the secret way out was
approached by a wall ladder, hooked into position, and
kept for emergency use during the days of air-raids.

Once on the roof, Pyne knew the way to a roof-light
which was covered with slates, making the hatch cover
seem like a part of the roof. The way up to this from inside was through a loft let in the ceiling of a cupboard; no
one but the Slob Mob had discovered it since the war.

He did not think the Chelham crowd would find where
it was.

Pyne neared the Club and saw that everything was as he
had left it, except that the policeman who had been
huddled against the wall was looking at him, eyes wide open,
a tie round his mouth gagging him effectively. Pyne went
towards him, and hope sprang into the man's eyes. Harry
stood close to him, and kicked him with scientific judgement
on the point of the jaw; the policeman lost consciousness.

There was a thumping sound from inside the Club, but
the steel shutters muffled most of the sound, and Pyne
could imagine that the little Australian and his friends
were having a council of war. He smiled that slow, evil
smile, the smile which had made Rollison, Nicholson and
others feel that this youth had a quality of evil which nothing could eradicate. He went to a trap door in the pavement by the side of the Club. He knew this trap door very

well. It led to the cellar, and in the days before the war it had been used for loading and unloading fuel for the central-heating plant. A long time ago, the coke-fired installation had been converted to gas, which was expensive when in use, but could be switched on and off so easily. The trap door was seldom used now.

Pyne rested the lid of the trap door against the wall, and shone his torch downwards. Against one wall was a perpendicular stairway, like that on board many ships, and rather like the ladders which led part of the way up tall chimneys. Pyne got his feet on this, and began to climb down backwards, leaving the door open so that he could get out quickly. There was a faint smell of gas; he knew what it was only too well, because he had made a slight fracture in one of the feed pipes earlier that evening. He waited for a moment in the cellar passage below, and could hear footsteps above his head. He switched on an electric light, which revealed the gas pipes, the hot water and the cold water pipes; the feeders for all the services led this way. He went along the wide passage to the alcove where the big gas heater was in position. It wasn't on tonight, and there was no sound down here except the footsteps above. He went close to the gas heater, and a strong smell of gas came. He went to a pipe on which he had been working that afternoon, knowing exactly what he wanted to do; the cleverest trick was to make it seem as if there had been an accidental fracture, and this was a flexible lead, which could be cut without the damage being immediately noticeable. He had started the cut with a nail file, and rubbed it with dirt afterwards; had it been discovered during the day, no one would have suspected sabotage. No one had discovered it, and Pyne knew quite well that there had been practically no chance that anyone would.

He liked to be careful, that was all.

He took the flexible pipe between his fingers, worked it up and down several times—and heard it snap. More gas whispered out, and he coughed and dodged back. Gas hissed out of the pipe like the threat of a snake. He coughed again, keeping the sound low.

Now he came to the most difficult task of all; how to ignite the gas without getting hurt himself, and without showing the slightest indication on his clothes or on his body that he had been near the scene of the explosion. A trail of petrol or of dynamite would be effective, but might be traced afterwards, and the essential thing about this was to make sure that the coroner's verdict was 'accidental death'. There was one way: the old-fashioned way; a firework of the slow burning kind. He took one from his pocket.

He turned his back on the main installation, breathing hard, reached the ladder, hauled himself through the trap door, and lit the firework. He waited long enough to close the door, and so keep the smell of gas in. One could never be sure, another policeman might pass, or a sailor returning from the docks the long way round. No one was about. The street lights burned dimly. He began to run, on his toes, and he reached Whale Street and the porch with the crashed van blocking it when a car swung into the road some distance along. Its headlights blazed along the street, shining on him, making it impossible for him to hide.

* * *

Rollison, in the Chelham flat, was working slowly at the necktie round his wrists. It had been a slow job, but now the pain was gradually easing from his stomach and he was getting back more control of his limbs. His wrists were throbbing and aching as he kept working, fingers could not keep up the effort much longer. He could not be sure whether his physical weakness was getting worse or better.

He managed to get the tie twisted round in such a way that he could pluck at the knot, but the knot itself was very tight. Had it been rope or cord, he could not have made more progress—but the knot *was* getting looser.

The danger now was that he might tighten it again.

He hooked his right thumb through the knot—and from that moment on it was only a matter of time; precious time.

It was another five minutes before he was free, and then his arms began to twitch, and sharp pains shot through his wrists. The pain was excruciating for a few seconds, but then began to ease.

Doris was across the room, staring at him.

He hauled himself to his feet as he undid his gag; everything he did took him so long, and Doris seemed to be urging:

"Hurry, hurry!"

He went across to her, and worked on the knot of the gag, thinking all the time about what he must do next.

Follow the others?

Or warn the police?

All his inclination was to follow, but he had to reject it. He couldn't drive safely for a long time, yet. Even if he got to Whale Street he wouldn't be able to take any part in the fight. He had to rely on someone else; and it had to be the police.

Nicholson might still be at the Yard.

Rollison needed a telephone.

He felt Doris's gag loosen, and said: "I'll—I'll be back." He stood up, and stepped towards the door. He was wobbly at the knees, but his mind was quite clear. He felt as if his right arm had been amputated, but that sensation should soon pass. He reasoned that if there had been a telephone here, Charley from the hospital would have used it, so there wasn't one in the house—certainly not in the flats, and as far as he could judge the whole house was turned into flats. He reached the top of the stairs. They seemed very steep, there was a danger that he would topple down them. He gripped the banister rail tightly, and went down one at a time. He was half way down when he heard a man speaking: and a moment later, a dog barked. He looked down the well of the staircase, and saw a foreshortened view of a man leading a frisking, yapping smooth-haired terrier on a lead.

He called: "Hello, there!"

His voice was little more than a croak, and the yapping dog and the man telling it to be quiet drowned the call. He tried to shout again, but there was no strength in his voice. He put his right hand to his pocket, managed to drag out a small handful of coins, and dropped them all. The man disappeared, the dog still yapping. Rollison watched the silver coins falling like huge rain drops and saw them bounce and roll about the floor. The dog, at the front door, had stopped yapping, and the tinkling sound came clearly.

The man said aloud: "What's that?"

The dog yapped.

"*Help!*" cried the Toff, huskily. "*Wait—a—minute!*"

For a moment, he thought he had failed. Then he saw the man come into sight again, looking upwards; at a sharp word of command the dog stopped yapping, and Rollison's voice was very clear.

"Must get to a telephone," he called. "Is there one here? Telephone."

Then he staggered and nearly lost his footing; and the man came hurrying upstairs, the yapping dog bounding after him, this new source of excitement overcoming disappointment. Rollison reached the next landing, and stayed there. As the man drew near him, shouting: "*Down, Pip, down!*" Rollison said clearly:

"I must talk to Scotland Yard at once. Have you a telephone?"

"In—in my flat," the man said quickly. "Who are you?" Then he broke off as if realising that questions were a waste of time. He turned round, took the Toff's left arm, and steadied him down the stairs.

Rollison wondered where the gang were at this moment; it must be nearly an hour since they had gone, and they could get a long way in an hour.

21

RAID

A LITTLE woman with frizzy grey hair was on the telephone, and Rollison felt his heart drop when he saw her there. Her husband said: "Got to call the police, Daisy," and the frizzy-haired woman looked at him as if she hadn't heard. "Daisy, we've an emergency call. We—"

"Oh, hello, Kathy darling!" the little woman cried into the telephone, and her face became radiant; she looked as if she was oblivious of her husband and the man beside him. "How are you, my dear? I've been so worried about you, I couldn't get hold of you all the evening. Are you all right? . . . You're not over-doing it now, are you?"

"Daisy! You can talk to Kathy later. I've got—"

"Now you be careful, dear, you mustn't go lifting things. You don't want anything to happen now that everything's gone so well this far, do you? What's that? Oh, really—"

"Daisy!"

"Eh? Oh, just a minute, dear, your father wants to say something . . . For goodness sake, don't shout at me like that, Tom!" the frizzy-haired woman snapped in a different tone, and radiance was driven out of her eyes by annoyance. "If I can't talk to my own daughter—"

"Daisy, can't you understand—"

"No! I'm talking to—"

The man stepped forward, snatched the telephone out of her hand, and said into it:

"Kathy, I've got an emergency call to make, your mother will call again in a few minutes." He put the telephone down while his wife glared, and looked as if she would come forward to snatch the instrument back. "We've got to call the police, have some sense," the man

said mildly, and then lifted the receiver and dialled Whitehall 1212.

Rollison said to the woman: "I'm afraid someone might
be murdered, it's very urgent."

"*Murdered?*"

"Or badly hurt."

"Scotland Yard?" asked the man, bluffly. "There's a
Mr Rollison, to talk to Detective Inspector Nicholson if
he's in, or else . . ."

A minute later, Rollison heard Nicholson's deep voice;
and within another minute, he knew that Nicholson
would put everything in hand without losing any time.
He himself could relax—except that it was the last thing
he wanted to do. The frizzy-haired woman was saying:
"I'm ever so sorry." The man was saying: "It's all right,
Daisy, I couldn't help it, could I?" Then there were
sounds outside, and footsteps sounded clearly in the hall.
Rollison looked round, and through the open door of this
ground floor flat, he saw Harrison of the *Evening Globe*.

"Ray!" he called.

"Who—" Harrison began, and then recognised Rollison
and came striding in. "What's on?" he demanded.
"One of the girls tipped me off that Lee's taking a crowd
somewhere, and told me you were still here."

"Just," said Rollison. "Is my car outside?"

"Yes—with four flat tyres," Harrison said.

"These teenagers are efficient, never doubt that," said
Rollison grimly. "Have you a cab?"

"Yes."

"Next stop, Whale Street," Rollison said, and hesitated,
looked at the grey-haired man with the strong face who
had helped him so promptly, smiled, and went on:

"There's a girl upstairs, tied hand and foot—don't
worry, she's not hurt. Will you—"

"Tom!" cried the frizzy-haired woman. "Don't just
stand there, go and see to that girl! Can't you see who it
is? It's Mr Rollison."

Five minutes later, Rollison sat back in a corner of the

taxi, his eyes half-closed. Harrison at least had the sense to keep quiet. The taxi-driver had been briefed and bribed, and was rattling along at at least fifty miles an hour. Rollison's head was aching, but he was feeling much better physically. For the rest, he was not so good. He had been compelled to leave the main work of rescue to the police, and had a feeling of deep frustration as well as disappointment. Success or failure could only be judged by his ability to stop Lee from leading this raid—which meant that he had failed utterly; the rest of the rescue work had to be done by others.

That was a bitter thing to accept.

"How are you feeling?" Harrison asked.

"Completely bushed," said Rollison, and hitched himself up and opened his eyes. They were already in the City, in five minutes they should be at Whale Street. Then he thought of Girodo's café. It would be worth stopping there to see how many of the Mob were present—that should give him some idea of the weight of the battle.

He took it for granted that the Slob Mob and the Chelham students would fight like any two gangs; that razors, bicycle chains, bricks, knives, and coshes would be used; and he hated to think of the Chelham students, unused to the tactics, to the violence, to the savagery that would rule. A high-powered whine sounded behind him, and two police cars flashed by; he saw Nicholson sitting in the back of the leading one, but Nicholson didn't glance his way.

"He's taken his time," said Harrison.

"Eh? Oh, he'd lay it on with the Division first," said Rollison. "You can't panic old Nick." He was surprised to find that he could speak and think of Nicholson almost in terms of affection. "Ray, we'll stop first at—"

"That café?"

"Thanks."

"Right," said Harrison, and tapped on the glass and gave the driver fresh orders. They bowled past Aldgate Pump and out of the stillness of the City itself into the brightness and the bustle of the East End. Even at this hour lights were blazing across the street, and police cars were drawn up near the café—including Nicholson's. Rollison saw the Yard man getting out.

The cabby twisted round in his seat:

"They're keeping traffic away from there, guv'."

"Slow down on this side of the street," Harrison ordered, and a moment later, he added: "They're all here, Rolly— or most of 'em are."

"What?"

"The café's packed with the Slob Mob, so they aren't fighting," Harrison said, and he sounded almost disappointed.

"That's something," conceded Rollison, and he watched, puzzled, as the door of the café opened and Nicholson stepped inside. As the taxi-driver slowed down, Rollison heard the strident ringing of a fire engine bell, and, for the first time, began to think that there might be more to worry about than a gang fight.

"Let's get on to Ebbutt's gymnasium," he said quickly. "Ebbutt will know what's on." He dropped back into his seat, and said to the driver: "Sorry to keep changing my mind. Blue Dog, Mile End Road, please."

"I know Ebbutt's place," the driver said.

He swung across the Mile End Road towards the Blue Dog, which was closed for the night; it was now twenty minutes to eleven. But lights shone at the wooden gymnasium behind it, and across the open front door in scarlet neon lighting were the words: *Ebbutt's Gym*. Percy Wrightson was looking out of the doorway, and he shouted something to a man inside, then approached, hurrying. Rollison got out of the taxi as Bill Ebbutt appeared in the doorway; he also came hurrying, which was a remarkable thing for so fat a man. At ten yards, Rollison could hear him wheezing.

"What's on, Bill?" Rollison called.

"Mr Ar, the Slob Mob trapped those kids in the Whale Street Club, and it's caught fire," said Ebbutt. "It's blazing already, some parts of it are nearly down. There's a rumour that the police nearly caught Harry Pyne, but he buried his knife in one of them, and got away."

*   *   *

Rollison felt the numbness of shock and horror. Whale Street was only a quarter of a mile from here, and when he turned his head he could see the glow in the sky. In the distance another fire engine sounded, and he could hear the roaring note of the engine, but fire engines would have little room to manœuvre near the club.

Harrison was saying: "My God, oh my God," over and over again.

Ebbutt said: "They won't have a chance, Mr Ar, not a chance in hell. That place'll go up like matchwood, and there must be fifty kids in it!"

"My God," said Harrison. "Oh, my God."

Rollison felt a sickening pressure of dismay and despair as he stared towards the Club, and as Ebbutt's words cut into his thoughts. All the horror of the situation came to him, made worse by a sense of utter hopelessness. Then into the vacuum of his mind there came a single recollection; the Slob Mob had a secret way out of that building.

As the recollection flooded in, he began to move. There was only one hope, and he had to try to strengthen it.

"Back to Girodo's café, Ray, quick," he said. He forgot his own physical weariness and rushed to the taxi, climbing in quickly, as Harrison called:

"What good—"

"You go to Whale Street, I'll join you there," Rollison shouted, and to the cabby: "That Aldgate café, get there as if your tail was burning!" He dropped back into his seat as the taxi-driver rammed in the gear. He saw Harrison, Ebbutt, and the others hurrying towards the side of the gymnasium, where Ebbutt kept his old car, incredibly a T-Model Ford. He felt the cab swing round three corners, going so fast that it was almost dangerous. It swung into the High Street; he saw the police cars near the café as well as a cordon of police directing traffic to the other side of the road, and keeping an excited crowd back. Two police stood in front of the taxi as it slowed down. Rollison put his face out of the window, and called:

"I'm Rollison. Mr Nicholson here?"

"I don't care who—" the first policeman began.

"Hold it, Bill," said the second man. "Yes, Mr Rollison, it's okay for you to pass." He stood aside quickly, and as the taxi went crawling towards the café, Rollison opened the door and jumped out. He saw Nicholson and two other plain-clothes men just inside the doorway of the café; there seemed no room for another one to squeeze in. Youths were sitting on chairs, on tables, on the counter, and many were standing. All of these were facing the three detectives, and Ginger King was in the middle, standing up defiantly.

There was no sign of Harry Pyne.

A policeman on duty outside the door barred Rollison's path; then recognised him, and said:

"Mr Nicholson expecting you, sir?"

"Yes," lied Rollison, and the man pushed the door open a few inches. One of Nicholson's men looked round, saw the newcomer, and beckoned.

Nicholson was saying:

"You bloody young fools, this is mass murder. Don't you understand? And what's more—" He broke off when he saw the gaze from all the youngsters switch towards the man behind him, looked round, and saw Rollison.

Rollison could see at once that Nicholson was at his wits end. His face was deathly white and his eyes had an unnatural brilliance; he was tormented by the horror of what was happening, and could think of nothing else.

"Now you see—" he began, but Rollison bumped against him deliberately, and stood facing the crowd.

He said: "Ginger, do you want to go down as the biggest killer in history?"

"Listen! That was an accident! We wouldn't—"

"Let's see if you've got any guts," Rollison said. "There is a secret way of getting into that club house—

you've used it for the past five years and no one knows it as well as you. How can we get the others out and save them from burning? Come on, let's hear from you—how can we get them out?"

There was a tense silence, which seemed to go on and on, although in fact it lasted only for a moment or two. Then Ginger King's eyes seemed to light up, he smacked a clenched hand into an open palm, and roared:

"We can get 'em out through the roof, Slobs. Let's show these coppers a thing or two. *Let's go!*" He jumped forward, and for a moment it looked as if Nicholson and his men would try to hold them back; but Nicholson stood to one side, shouting an order to the constables in the entrance. Rollison was pushed back against the wall as Ginger King tore out of the café, his followers behind him, youths and girls tearing into the High Street, then along towards the parked cars, the motor-cycles, the scooters. The street echoed to the roar and rasp of engine starting, and the stench of exhaust was foul, but machines roared off, scooters with three and four youths up, the cars crazily overcrowded, too.

Nicholson said to the Toff: "Come on."

22

RESCUE WORKERS

As Rollison looked out of the Yard car towards the end of Whale Street, he saw the glow of the fire, which seemed to have started from the ground floor; the upper storey was smouldering now. Great billows of smoke were rising though, all red-tinged. He could see three fire engines jammed into the end of the street, where there was hardly room for them, and the firemen with their snaking hoses had difficulty in manœuvring. Jets of water were pouring and hissing on to the roof and the walls, but the fire was inside, and the great difficulty was to get through the steel shutters. Firemen were working on them desperately, two men were using oxy-acetylene burners to cut the metal, but the difficulty was to find room to move.

None of the Slob Mob's cars or motor-cycles were in sight, it would be a waste of time coming down here. But suddenly there was a burst of shouting, and a man called an order over the loud speaker.

"Let them pass. It's okay!"

Rollison got out of the car. At least two hundred people were jamming this end of the street, and the police were trying to force them back, but everyone was intent on the fire and the red-tinged smoke. Then the Slob Mob spilled into the far end of the street, clambering over the fire engines, the houses, the over-turned cars, and began to swarm along the blocked passage. Rollison saw some of them shinning up drain pipes. Firemen ran ladders up to the roof, and the youths climbed up as if they had been used to the trick all their lives. Figures appeared, angled against the roof and the skyline. It was impossible to distinguish one from another, there seemed so many of them. Men started shouting, and a fire engine turn-table was manœuvred closer to the club house roof.

Rollison said: "Can we get on that roof?"

"Better watch from here," said Nicholson.

"There's the old Warman warehouse," one of the Divisional men said. "We could go up there." He and Nicholson went first, Rollison followed, Harrison was just behind them. They pushed their way towards the corner where the biggest crowd had gathered. The Slob Mob youths were nearly all on the roof, a few were still shinning up the drain pipes—less agile but quite as ready to try. Voices sounded from the roof. Small figures were standing there gesticulating, next to firemen wearing steel helmets. The smell of smoke was harsh and thick, a lot of people were coughing.

The local detective led the way through a corner house, then across a little back yard towards the warehouse which overlooked the Whale Street Club from two streets away. It was a good viewpoint, but too far off to be of use to the firemen. They clattered up wooden staircases to the top floor, then up a loft ladder out on to the roof. Slates were cracking and breaking underfoot. The smoke seemed to be blowing the other way and the air was clearer up here. They could see the angry red of the fire, mostly near the ground; none had yet started to shoot through the roof of the old building.

Harrison exclaimed: "*Look at them.*"

Rollison stood with a hand against a chimney breast, watching the scene, knowing that the others were as astonished, perhaps more astonished, than he. For the Slob Mob and some firemen were breaking open a hole in the roof of the Whale Street Club. The frame of a rooflight appeared, obviously the secret entrance. Youth after youth lowered himself at the end of ropes, and youth after youth was hauled up towards the roof. Firemen did most of the carrying from there. Chelham youths overcome by the fumes and smoke were passed from man to man across the roof until they were on the turn-table, and other firemen carried them down. Cameras were flashing, and a newscamera had reached the spot. Now and again a ragged cheer rose as someone else was lowered safely to the ground. The police had cleared a channel for ambulances, but most of the rescued youths were laid along the pavement, and obviously few of them were hurt; some began to move and talk and shout.

Rollison watched the roof most of the time.

There were the members of the Slob Mob, some still down below, some on the roof, working as if their own lives were at stake; tearing at the job with as much single-mindedness, as much courage, and as much desperation as firefighters had fought during the air-raids. These were youths to whom war was only a word, Hitler a name, bombs a thing to see on television or on the cinema screen.

A sudden glow of light spread from the biggest hole made in the roof, and the cheers changed to gasps of alarm. A tongue of flame shot out. Harrison turned and said: "I've got to reach a telephone," and he hurried away. Rollison, the Yard man, and an Inspector from the Division stood and watched as firemen and mobsters worked with even greater fury and frenzy against a deepening background of fiery red. The billowing smoke swept down on Rollison now, but he hardly noticed it; he simply stood and watched until he saw that the youths were coming up on their own, two and three at a time, hauling themselves over with the help of ropes. No one else was carried. Men on the roof were shouting, others were bending down, trying desperately to give help to more of the Mob—and suddenly Rollison saw Ginger King dragged up throught the hole, *with his hair alight.*

A fireman smothered Ginger with a cloth; a moment later the cloth was drawn off, and someone tried to help Ginger away. He pushed them aside, went back to the hole, and looked down. Then he waved his arms in a scissors motion as if to signify that everything was over, and turned back and clambered over the roof. The firemen on the turn-table shouted through the loud speaker, and Rollison heard the cry:

"That's the lot. The place will collapse in a minute. Get everyone away."

Police began to clear the street. Firemen worked madly to get the youths away—and Rollison saw members of the Slob Mob picking up some of the Chelham students and carrying them over their shoulders towards safety. Some of the South West London students were walking away by themselves, a few were being helped. As they went away, the firemen moved their equipment, and police began to manhandle cars, so as to get them clear before the building collapsed. A single high-pitched whistle brought a silence among the men, broken only by the roaring of the fire, and a man called clearly:

"Drop everything. Get out of range."

Rollison watched the orderly exodus, and, ten minutes later, saw the roof of the Whale Street Club collapse and drop into the inferno below.

Nicholson said, in a gruff voice: "I wonder if anyone was left inside."

* * *

As far as it was possible to tell, everyone had been brought out. No one could be positive until the morning, but the coach drivers said that their total load had been eighty-three, and seventy-five went back into the coaches, two hours after the collapse of the Club, when eight were already in hospital. Five broken legs, three cases of superficial burning, one case of crushed ribs, and three broken arms made up the tally of the night's injuries. No one on either side was dead or likely to die.

"What I want to know is what's going to happen now," Nicholson said, heavily. "I'm prepared for anything, but I'll be happier when we've got the man Pyne."

"Yes," Rollison said, absently. He was standing next to Nicholson by a police car; a telephone kiosk light glowed nearby.

"I know one thing."

Rollison forced himself to grin and to say: "Only one?"

"That's not funny," Nicholson growled. "I know that

if you hadn't gone to the café and talked to Ginger King, the Slobs wouldn't have done it. If I'd stayed there five more minutes I'd have had them so scared that all they would have thought about was saving themselves from a lifer. What I don't understand," went on the Yard man, and his tone as well as his words took on the familiar but unwanted pomposity, "is how it is that an individual with your background and social environment can understand these people so well, whereas I, who come from the same social stratum so to speak, don't understand them at all."

Rollison said: "Nice of you, Nick, but it doesn't make me feel good."

"The more I think about it, the more I think you did the only possible thing in the beginning," said Nicholson. "I am serious about that, Mr Rollison. To have rejected all the Chelham overtures would have been a mistake, too, and to have talked of forming a club in the normal sense would have been ridiculous. Price's death was bad enough, but the situation could have been much worse. One thing stands out very clearly, though."

Rollison was thinking of Harry Pyne, as he said:

"It isn't over yet."

"We still have to catch the one man and according to my information seven of the members of the Slob Mob did not follow Ginger King. It can be assumed that some of those were afraid, and the others were likely to take Pyne's side. However, the thing I was referring to is this, Mr Rollison: put the two groups side by side, the Chelham students and the Slob Mob, and there really isn't much difference between them."

"Happy thought," said Rollison. "A very happy thought. Any possibility of proving that Pyne started the fire?"

"I should think so," answered Nicholson. "One of the Divisional men was tied up and left near the front porch, and he saw Pyne come back—in fact Pyne kicked him into unconsciousness. A man also recognised Pyne, who

came here alone after the rest of the Mob had gone. The
fire started soon afterwards. We'll get Pyne for it."

"Ah," said Rollison. "Good." He pushed a hand
across his forehead, and said: "Think I could get a lift
back to my flat?"

"Yes, of course," said Nicholson. "I'll arrange it at
once, Mr Rollison. And before you go I would like to say
again that I don't think I shall ever be able to understand
you, but I do now understand how you got your reputation."

"Oh, nonsense," said Rollison. "Before I go, I'll
'phone Jolly, too."

Jolly was not only awake, but answered so quickly that
he must have been waiting by the telephone.

Rollison asked the police car to drop him at the end of
Gresham Terrace, and the driver did so. He stepped out
of the car, and said good night although it was now nearly
four o'clock in the morning. He looked along the street.
The stars seemed very bright, the roofs seemed very high;
these were palaces compared with the Whale Street
hovels. Rollison walked slowly towards Number 22g,
keeping a very close watch on the doorways leading to it,
and expecting Harry Pyne; but there was no sign of man
or movement. He reached the doorway of his house, and
hesitated. There was a light on at his living-room window; he smiled to himself. Nothing would have made
Jolly go to bed until he returned. He took out his key and
turned it in the lock. There was just a possibility that
Pyne was hiding across the road, a possibility too that he
had forced his way in here, and was waiting inside.

Rollison heard the lock click.

He pushed the door an inch or two, and then coughed;
and afterwards he listened to the intense silence. There
was no sound, and he could not make out the noise of
anyone breathing. He pushed the door wide. The light
from a street lamp shone into the hall. He pushed the
door right back against the wall, and made sure that no
one was hiding behind it. There was a possibility that

Pyne was lurking further up the stairs, but also that he had not come here at all—he might think that it was the one place where the police were bound to come. Rollison closed the door slowly behind him, and stood in the darkness for a moment—the only light came from the landing at his floor. He listened intently as he moved forward, reached the foot of the stairs, and still heard nothing. There was nowhere to hide except in shadowy corners, he reminded himself, and switched on a brighter light at the landing above. The shadows disappeared. There was no sign of the youth, or those who had stayed with him. Rollison had prepared himself for this final clash unnecessarily. He—

He heard a tiny sound, behind him; as of metal on metal. He stopped at the foot of the stairs. The sound was repeated, and there came the creak of the front door, opening. Then it banged back. Rollison heard a scrabble of footsteps, saw three or four shapes outlined against the street light—and saw two knives, hurtling towards him, chest high.

23

FOUR TO ONE

ROLLISON could not distinguish one figure from another, could not be sure which was Pyne, but those knives meant just one thing: this was the expected attempt at final retribution. He was on the turn, as they came towards him—and he jumped forward. Sight of him doing that must have astounded them; even as he moved, he sensed the astonishment, the momentary pause in their actions. Then Pyne said viciously:

"Get him!"

Rollison felt the first knife stab against his clothes, jar against the steel vest, and catch in the cloth. He snatched it out by the handle, before it dropped. He was still going forward. He saw that Pyne was the nearest of the four men, and Pyne had a knife in his hand, the light from the landing glinted on it—but Pyne had not dreamed of facing a charging man with a knife, and he lost a fraction of a second. Rollison struck at his wrist, caught his knuckles, made the knife fall. He flung his own knife into the shoulder of a man who had swung round, and then he closed with Pyne, anticipating exactly what tactics Pyne would use. The man's knee came up, towards his groin, but Rollison thrust his left hand down against the rising knee, so that Pyne was thrown suddenly off his balance, a long way from his objective. Rollison sent him staggering back against the others, then lunged forward, grabbed Pyne round the waist, and hoisted him off his feet. Rollison hurled him bodily at the men behind, heard Pyne scream, knew that he had impaled himself on the knife in one man's hand. He saw two of them turning and running out of sight, but one was on the ground just outside, with Pyne on top of him. Rollison bent down and grabbed Pyne's coat lapels and hoisted him to his feet as the other youth struggled to get up. He flung Pyne on to the youth. As they collapsed, there was a flurry of footsteps from the stairs above Rollison's head, unfamiliar footsteps which gave him a moment of dread—but as he turned round, he saw Jonas Lee and two more of the Chelham students leaping down the stairs. One of them yelled: "*Hi, Toff!*" and pushed past him, leapt over Pyne and the other youth and went racing along the street in the wake of the two who had run away.

Jonas Lee stood over Pyne and his crony, then he looked up into Rollison's face and said:

"Four to one. Not bad odds, Toff."

"Thanks for coming," Rollison said, breathlessly.

"You don't need to thank us," Jonas declared. "You could take 'em, two to one, four to one, ten to one. We all under-estimated you, Mr Toff." There was a hint of rough laughter in the Australian's voice—and it vanished when Pyne began to move. He bent down, astride Pyne, grasped the other's head between his hands, raised it, and thumped it down on the pavement; once. Pyne groaned. A dozen other youths might have gone on smacking the man's head against the pavement, but Jonas Lee simply let it go, and inquired: "We learning, Toff?"

"We're all learning," Rollison said. "Has anyone sent for the police?"

"Your Jolly wallah did the moment we heard trouble," said Jonas. "He's a right good 'un, Jolly. Let me tell you something else: he told us what you are wearing under your shirt—there isn't a knife in the East End that would carve through it. What was that I said about you? Always be prepared. That's about right." Jonas was talking in short, jerky sentences, and grinning as he did so. "That's the Toff all right. In two words. Always prepared. Did you expect this?"

"Yes," said Rollison.

"Been disappointed if it hadn't happened, eh? Why not make sure the police followed you? Or that Jolly was waiting with one of those tear-gas phials?"

"Don't you know?" asked Rollison.

"If I knew I wouldn't ask."

"You've got something there," said Rollison. "All right, Jonas, I'll tell you. I wanted to make sure I could still handle the Pynes of this world by myself. Jolly, Inspector Nicholson, and anyone else with any sense would say that it was sheer bravado, or even worse, conceit. You can probably understand what made it vital."

After a long pause, Jonas said slowly: "I get it. The man who'll never grow old. That's our Toff." He looked at the passage, and Rollison turned to look round too. Jolly was coming along, not hurrying, obviously content that Rollison was unhurt.

As Jolly reached the hall a car swung into the street, and before he reached the doorway, the police were getting out of the car and bearing down on Pyne. Further along Gresham Terrace, two of the Chelham students were bringing one of the Slob Mob back; the fourth youth had escaped.

"But it wasn't a bad bag," said Jonas Lee, cheerfully, and stifled a yawn. "Think I'd better go and get some rest, Mr Rollison. Er—thanks. I really mean that." He hesitated, and then gave a broad grin and said: "You're the tops, Toff. Good-o!"

He turned and went off . . .

Rollison was smiling as he went upstairs, with Jolly behind him, to find his bed turned down and his pyjamas laid out, and a tray with a hot milk drink ready for him. He stared at the milk. He grinned. He sipped, and then drank with relish. He yawned as he undressed, looked at the red bruises where the knives had struck him, and said to Jolly:

"Very effective vest still, Jolly."

"But useless had the Mob used guns, sir."

"Ever known an East End mob use guns?" inquired Rollison, and scowled. "All right, there might come a time, but I don't think it will be yet; I think we're in for a period of armistice in the gang wars, too. If the police play their hand properly, and I think they will, this could do a lot of good."

"A great deal of good indeed, sir," said Jolly. "Now I think you would be wise to get some rest. The police and the Press will be bound to start worrying you first thing in the morning."

"Keep 'em at bay," urged Rollison.

When he was fully awake, a little after noon the next day, he was not surprised to learn that Jolly had acted as watchdog. The police, newspapermen, and members of the Chelham students had already been here; they were coming back during the afternoon. They had left news for the Toff, however, including the fact that Doris Evans was now completely recovered, that all of the Chelham students had been accounted for, that all but two of the Slob Mob were accounted for, also—and that it was known that these two were Harry Pyne men, and both in hiding.

Pyne and the men who had raided the Gresham Terrace house were already under remand, in custody, on a charge of inciting to violence and causing grievous bodily harm to Alec Price. More serious charges would come later. The Divisional police were gathering more evidence against Pyne, but according to a note from Nicholson, none of the Slob Mob had said a word against Pyne or his cronies.

"As a matter of fact," Nicholson said, when he called at half past two, "they have behaved in a much better way than I expected. Usually when you get a mob like that, several of them begin to squeal and squeak the moment there's a break-up, but no one has. Ginger King gave the word, and they're doing what he tells them."

"There's more in our Ginger than Harry Pyne thought," remarked Rollison, thoughtfully. "No one squeal on Pyne?"

"Not in his mob, but we'll get him for Price's death— which might possibly be brought in as manslaughter. We'll get a couple of the other brutes, too!"

"How about the Chelham crowd?" asked Rollison. "Are you going to take any action?"

"That's one of the things I was going to talk to you about, sir. Obviously they caused a breach of the peace, although there was no actual fighting—the Slob Mob laid everything on before the Chelham crowd arrived. Some of the Chelham leaders could be charged with behaviour calculated to cause a breach of the peace, but there is a feeling among my superiors that it would be a mistake, especially as the youth Price has died from his injuries. I can't be sure that my advice will be taken, sir, but I did make it clear that I proposed to have a word with you."

Rollison said, warmly: "Nick, you're ten times the man I thought you were. I'd have two or three of them in court—and two or three of Ginger King's special friends in the Slob Mob, too."

"You would, sir?"

"Provided you could be reasonably sure that the magistrate would bind 'em all over—except anyone known to have attacked young Alec Price," said Rollison. "Everyone knows the facts, no one is going to blame anyone else. If they got off without any charges at all it might go to their heads. If they all get a wigging from the magistrate and let off with a caution, it might impress them with the fact of equal justice in Bethnal Green and Chelham, which would be a good thing."

"I'll certainly put this to my superiors, sir," said Nicholson.

Ray Harrison telephoned, just after Nicholson had gone. He had been sent to cover a case in Devon, so he couldn't get in to congratulate the Toff, but—well, he hoped his story in the *Evening Globe* would say thanks for him. It covered much of the front page, and it included a graphic action sketch of Rollison being the target for a dozen throwing knives, all of them sticking into his clothing as he rushed forward into the attack; and just above his head was the figure of the man without a face, that sign of the Toff.

Even Jolly was amused.

There followed a trail of youngsters, from Chelham and

from the East End, most tongue-tied, all of them fascinated by the Trophy Wall, all of them wanting to know what souvenir he would have of this affair. He said that it wasn't over yet, and that he would ask for suggestions later, and so sent them off in high good humour.

Next morning, after Pyne had been committed for trial by jury, Ginger King, Luigi Girodo, and Smith were charged with causing a breach of the peace, alongside Jonas Lee, Anne Darby, and the youth named Charley, perhaps the smallest of the three. The local police gave evidence. The coach drivers gave evidence, so did several local residents: and it was established that Pyne alone had started the fire. The magistrate at the East End Court was an elderly man with a wealth of experience. He could remand the accused for a week for a Probation Officer's report, or to a higher court, he could sentence them to fine or imprisonment, or he could bind them over to be of good behaviour for twelve months or more. Rollison watched the six accused from the back of the court, and he could tell that Jonas Lee and Ginger King were the most nervous there. King had cause to be.

The magistrate said: "Whenever I see a mixture of good and evil, as I have seen in your behaviour, I think the good should have its chance to come out on top. So I am going to bind all of you over to keep the peace for twelve months. You understand that if any one of you should break that order you may be brought back and sentenced for your part in this disgraceful affair. You would be dealt with with particularly severity." He looked straight at King. "Do you understand?"

"Yessir."

"I hope you do. I am giving you this chance because it is evident that you were unaware of much that others in this—ah—gang were doing, and because you showed remarkable bravery during the work of rescue." The magistrate looked at Lee.

"Do you understand what I have said?"

"Yes, sir."

"You?"

He was answered six times before nodding dismissal, and Rollison saw the relief in the eyes of Ginger King and Jonas Lee. He was outside the court when they came out of another entrance, and Jonas Lee looked up at him with a cheeky grin and said:

"We're going to have a cuppa at Girodo's café. Coming, Mr Toff?"

"I shall get into trouble with Jolly if I don't go home soon," Rollison said. "We'll have a celebration party later." Solemnly—as solemnly as Nicholson, he reminded himself—he shook hands with each of them, the last being Ginger King. He grinned at Ginger, and said:

"You and Jonas could tear this town apart if you set your minds to it, Ginger—you could also put a lot of it together so that it will never fall apart. Why don't you talk it over with Jonas?"

"That's just what we'll do, Mr Rollison," Ginger said.

Rollison drove off in his sand-and-blue Bentley, the tyres inflated again, watched by all the group and their friends, who had gone there to hear the court decision. He did not go straight home, after all, but to Bill Ebbutt's gymnasium. Bill was in a state almost of exaltation, and took Rollison's arm and led him towards one of the three rings, in a corner, and said:

"Just watch that boyo's right, Mr Ar. Looks like a broom-stick, but—" he broke off, drew in a wheezy breath, and said: "*See!*" A skinny arm from a midget boy shot out, and a youth fell heavily to the canvas. "Gee, that boy's going to be a world-beater," Ebbutt declared, and wheezed and grumbled, and then started, looked round at Rollison, and asked: "What can I do for you, Mr Ar? That was a bloody good show you put up lars night, and you've only got to say the word. What'll it be?"

"Think you could stage some exhibition bouts and a match between Ginger King's Slobs and the Chelham students? It would do both sides a lot of good."

"It's as good as done," said Ebbutt, and enthusiasm

shrilled into his voice. "What's more we could give the funds to those who got hurt in the fire, do a bitta good and show them the way to go about things. Sure, I'll fix it. You going to suggest it to them?"

"No, Bill. You are."

"Just leave it to me," said Ebbutt.

*   *   *

It was two days later when Jonas Lee, Doris Evans, Anne Darby, and Ginger King—the sole representative of the Slob Mob—called to see the Toff. Ginger had spruced himself up for the occasion. His charred hair was plastered down as sleekly as it would go, he was wearing a new suit, and a collar and a tie; he looked a little comical, but no one seemed to think so. He kept next to Doris Evans, and now and again he glanced at Doris as if at his own personal property.

Jonas had fallen back into his mood of tongue-tied 'embarrassment'. Anne Darby said very little, simply, how much they wanted to thank the Toff.

"Forget it," he disclaimed cheerfully. "The boot's on the other foot."

"No, it isn't, Mr Rollison," said Doris Evans, "and you know it isn't. We—er—we really came to ask you for another favour."

"Oh?"

"You know the man Ebbutt, don't you?" asked Doris, and Rollison nodded and Ginger King smothered a grin. King had so many freckles that it was hard to believe that there was anything basically vicious in him; the freckles made him look so much a boy. "Well, he's suggested a boxing match," Doris said, "and we've agreed. We wondered if you would act as master of ceremonies."

"There's nothing I'd like more," said Rollison. "Good old Bill Ebbutt!"

"Good old Toff," said Ginger King, expansively and unexpectedly. "Go on, Dorry, get it out." He slid an arm round Doris's waist. "He won't bite you."

Doris laughed.

"I'm not so sure," she said. "Ebbutt suggested that we might put the proceeds from the match to help those who got injured in the fire, but they're all covered by the Health Service, and we happen to know none of them will lose much by it, so we thought we would make this the first leg of a fund to build a club-house near the Elephant and Castle. There's a plot of ground available, and it's about half way between Whitechapel and Chelham. Both sides would use the club, and—"

She broke off.

"Blimey, she's proper nervous," Ginger said, and gave her a squeeze. "We want to call it Toff House, Mr Rollison. Any objections?"

After a long pause, Rollison said very softly: "No, Ginger, I haven't, but I want a brick from the first lot delivered to the site, to add to my trophies." He paused again, and grinned, and demanded: "Any objections?"

"Just show me anyone who'll object," Ginger said, "and I'll deal with him."

"Whose job are you pinching?" Jonas Lee demanded.

*   *   *

The first stone at Toff House was laid exactly three months later. It so happened that it was in the same week that Harry Pyne was sentenced to two concurrent terms of seven years imprisonment for his part in the fire and for manslaughter of Alec Price; and his cronies were sentenced to five years.

That evening, Rollison believed, Ginger King and his Slobs were a little more thoughtful than usual, but Ginger did not brood for long. He was too busy telling Jonas Lee how little he knew about bricklaying, and Jonas was too busy telling Ginger that he couldn't saw a piece of wood in two with a straight line if he tried.

THE END